the
Wave

*Maria —
The world is an amazing
place. Be curious about it!
Freddie Remza
2011*

Freddie Remza

Outskirts Press, Inc.
Denver, Colorado

Ride the Wave
All Rights Reserved.
Copyright © 2011 Freddie Remza
v4.0

Cover Photo © 2011 JupiterImages Corporation. All rights reserved - used with permission.

Outskirts Press, Inc.
http://www.outskirtspress.com

ISBN: 978-1-4327-6642-9

Library of Congress Control Number: 2010942959

Outskirts Press and the "OP" logo are trademarks belonging to Outskirts Press, Inc.

PRINTED IN THE UNITED STATES OF AMERICA

Dedication

Ride the Wave is a story about friendship and change. With her friends' support, Shelly is better able to handle any situation that comes her way. I, too, have an amazing set of friends. Please know that each of you, in your own special way, has helped me ride the waves. So to you, my dear friends, I dedicate this book.

Freddie

Acknowledgements

Special thanks go to Ian and Claire Wallace of Cape Town, South Africa for assisting me in the research of this book. I'm very grateful for the time they spent sharing their knowledge and showing me around their amazing country.

Part One

New York

"The only way to make sense out of change is to plunge into it, move with it, and join the dance."

Alan Watts
(1915-1973)
British philosopher, writer

Chapter One
Nothing Ever Stays the Same

"Shelly, whatcha thinking about?" asked Amy pulling me out of my trance.

I turned my head from the window. "Nothing much, just wondering how it must feel to be a pumpkin. You know, one day everyone is excited about you. They carve a funny face and place you in a special spot in the window so you're admired by the world. Then a couple weeks later you're tossed outside, ignored, and ready for the compost pile."

"You can be so weird," Amy laughed. "How do you come up with this stuff?"

"It's a gift I have," I laughed as I pointed out the window. "See that decayed pumpkin abandoned over there amongst the pile of leaves?"

"What about it?"

"It reflects my mood. Amy, don't you hate riding this bus?"

"No kidding, but what's the alternative?"

"Absolutely none. Won't turn sixteen until June and riding with other kids is out."

"Yeah, parents can be weird about those kinds of things. Anyway, next year this time we'll have wheels."

I looked over at her and smiled.

"What?" Amy asked.

"You know, I've known you since first grade and not much has changed."

Amy scrunched her eyebrows and looked directly into my eyes. "Is that good or bad?"

"Definitely good—you have this way of finding something positive out of any bad situation. Doesn't anything rattle you?"

"I try to look at the bright side of things. Don't be such a worry wart."

"So that's what you think I am, a worry wart?"

"Well, sort of…okay, big time!" Amy laughed. "Hey, not to change the subject, but what about the school play? Going out for it?"

"Yeah, auditions start after school on Monday," I answered as I continued to stare out the bus window.

"Which role are you going for?" asked Amy.

"Hermia—she's the daughter of Egeus who's upset because she won't marry the guy her father picked out. Instead she wants to marry Lysander."

"Wicked," Amy replied.

"Yeah, I hope I get a speaking part instead of queen of costumes and props like last year in *The Tempest*."

"Ahh, remember…think positive. Besides, with this your second year at Jackson High, you should have a better chance. What's the play?" Amy asked placing her backpack on the floor.

"*A Midsummer Night's Dream*," I replied feeling quite amused over this conversation. "You know Amy, there's nothing more exciting than performing under those bright lights. I can't see the audience but occasionally a cough or laugh can be heard. The applause tops everything. It makes all those rehearsals worth it."

"I know. I've never been in a play, but I experienced that on the soccer field. I love the electricity that fills the air when a ball finds its way into the goal from the side of my foot. Magic! Anyway, most likely I won't see much of you once rehearsals start."

"Look at all the times you stayed after school for practices and games," I quickly threw back at her.

"All right, all right! So tell me, do you have any plans for Saturday? Want to go to the mall and later take in a movie? My mom said she'd drive."

"I can't," I said. "Tomorrow is Mei's Gottcha Day. We're doing some kind of family thing with her. It's been five years since we brought her home."

"Five years? I remember the day you heard about your parents' plan to adopt Mei."

"Yeah, I guess I was pretty strung out about it."

"Strung out? You had one major spas attack, girl!"

"Come on Amy, give me some slack. I was only ten at the time. The thought of having a sister didn't fit into my plan."

"So what changed your mind?"

"I don't know. I guess a lot of different things. Seeing you excited about it kind of rubbed off. Then my mom explained how Chinese orphanages were overflowing with little girls. That got to me. Eventually I realized my selfishness."

"Your family waited forever to get Mei," said Amy.

"Actually, the wait lasted a little over a year, but Mrs. Presley told my mom that things have really changed."

"How come?" asked Amy.

"China tightened its adoption policies. I think the country realized there was a shortage of girls; so in some parts of China, couples were allowed two kids. Oh look, my stop." I picked up my bag and worked my way out of my seat. "Give me a call tonight."

I walked the short distance to my house before I spotted Mei playing with her friend, Jennifer.

"Shelly," Mei yelled when she saw me walking up the driveway. "You're home!" I smiled as she ran toward me and grabbed my hand. "Hi Mei, how was kindergarten today?"

"Good, guess what? We made these turkeys and then wrote down something we're thankful for."

"We did that, too!" Jennifer chimed in.

"Yeah, I think lots of kids do that around Thanksgiving. What did you write?"

"I said my mommy, daddy and sister," Mei announced with a toothless grin.

"Thanks, Mei. You know, I'm glad I have you for a sister, too." I gave her hand a little squeeze. Mei looked up at me and sported the shy smile she often gave when she didn't know what to say. She giggled, took off, and raced Jennifer to the backyard. Mei's birth took place in China but she unquestionably was American. No matter, my parents continuously exposed her to the culture of her birth country.

"Mom, I'm home," I yelled as I entered the house.

"I'm upstairs," Mom yelled back.

I took off my jacket and allowed my nose to follow the trail to the baked brownies cooling on the kitchen counter.

After cutting a generous portion, I pulled the freshly printed script out of my bag.

"Hi, Shelly, how did your day go?" Mom asked as she walked into the kitchen and spotted me eating my brownie. "Just have one of those, please. I have a chicken in the oven. Dad doesn't have an afternoon class today so we're having an early dinner."

"How come?" I asked.

"He's taking his students to the town meeting on Monday instead."

"Is that the group pushing to save the bog on Cranberry Hill Road?" I asked.

"The same—Dad's objective is to involve his students with environmental issues right from the start instead of just reading about them."

"Ah huh, he's been working on that project for awhile."

"You know, Shelly, why don't you consider going with them."

"What would I do there? They're all graduate students."

"It might be interesting to see a citizens' action group at work."

"Yeah, I know but I have a lot of stuff going on right now," I said looking down at my lines.

"Okay, but you'll be missing a great opportunity. Did you see Mei when you got off the bus?"

"She's outside with Jennifer."

"What's that you're looking at—your script?"

"Ah huh. I'm learning these lines for my audition on Monday."

"Let me know if you need help," Mom offered as she opened the oven door to check on the chicken.

"Thanks, but right now I need to memorize this

Shakespearean English. It's a little hard—words like *art thou* and *thy*—stuff like that." I looked up from my script and found Mom smiling at me. "What's so funny?" I asked.

"Oh, just thought back to the time when you gave this report. I think you were in fifth grade. Remember how nervous you were?"

"How could I forget that?" I said as I took the last bite of my brownie.

"You called it your day of terror," Mom reminded me. "Now look, here you are auditioning for the lead part in a play. You've come a long way, Shelly."

"I guess so." I pushed the chair back and stood up. "One thing I've discovered, Mom, is nothing ever stays the same."

Chapter Two
A Great Opportunity

Nothing ever stays the same...little did I realize the reality of those words. Very little time passed when Dad came home looking quite excited. He plucked a letter down on the table and announced, "Kathy, I have fantastic news about my sabbatical next year."

"What's a sab er a sabaco, what's it called again, Daddy?" Mei asked as she sat down at the table.

"Hi Mei. It's called a sabbatical. That's when you get time off from teaching," Dad laughed. He walked over and gave Mei a peck on the cheek.

"Oh, like a vacation?"

"No, it's not meant to be that. I can use this sabbatical to do research, write a book, or take part in some type of activity that keeps me up-to-date in my teaching."

Mom placed the chicken on the table and scooped a spoonful of peas onto Mei's plate. Mei hated peas and always buried them under her mashed potatoes. I felt Mom knew she did that even though she never said anything.

Mom sat down next to Mei and asked, "So tell me, Steve? What's your great opportunity?"

"Do you remember the application I submitted last spring to the University of Cape Town? Well, I've been accepted."

Mom stopped eating and put her fork down next to her plate. She placed her hand under her chin and said, "You got the position? Oh!"

Dad answered, "Yeah, I felt things went well after my phone interview with them a couple of months ago."

"But then nothing more happened," Mom said. "I figured it was a dead issue and you would use the sabbatical to finish writing the book you started."

"I admit, after they checked out my credentials with the university and then never called back . . . well, I figured they decided on someone else."

Dad was excited, but Mom clearly looked upset. She didn't totally react because of Mei and me sitting there, but her doom and gloom facial expression gave it away. Did I really want to be clued in on this? It might be great news for Dad, but it didn't sound like a great coming attraction for the rest of us.

In a reassuring voice Dad said, "It's only for a year, Kathy. Think what a great experience it'll be for the family."

"Do you really think so, Steve?" Mom asked.

"Hey guys, where are we going?" Mei blurted out. By now she had her peas totally hidden inside the potatoes. This, however, appeared not to be a primary concern for Mom— Mei not eating her peas.

I could no longer stand the suspense so I asked, "Where's this University of Cape Town? Is it far?"

Dad looked over at me and said, "You might say that, Shelly. It's in South Africa."

Did I hear that correctly?

"South Africa! You mean Cape Town, South Africa? You've got to be kidding! Do we HAVE to go? What about my friends, school and…and the PLAY? I'm all set to audition for the play! I don't want to move to South Africa."

"Now, Shelly, let's be calm about this," Dad answered. "We won't be going until the summer after you've completed your sophomore year. They have English speaking schools in Cape Town that you and Mei can attend. We'll return in time for you to finish your senior year at Jackson."

"But why? Why are you going there?" I asked.

"To do research on global warming," Dad said.

"You mean you'll be quitting your job at the university?" I said as I felt a hot flush come over me.

"No, that's what the sabbatical is for."

I looked over at Mom and she stared back. Then she looked over at Dad and said, "Steve, never did I think this would really happen."

"Kathy, we talked about this. You seemed okay with the idea." Dad reached over for the chicken and dropped two pieces onto his plate.

"Well, to be honest with you, when you first mentioned this I didn't think it would fly. It seemed so far fetched. And if I recall, I never said I liked the idea. Matter of fact, the way I remembered that conversation, I didn't say anything at all."

Dad took a bite of his potatoes. "Well, you should have. Kathy, I'll be working at the oldest university in South Africa. Global warming and its effects on South African agriculture and its wildlife population are all major concerns.

Participating as part of the research team is an opportunity I find hard to pass up."

"What about me?" I asked as he tried to soft soap this whole thing.

Dad looked at me and winked. "Living in another part of the world and experiencing a different culture will be part of you forever, Shelly. Right now you may not see the advantages, but later you will."

"Are we going to China?" Mei asked.

Mom answered, "No, honey. It's called South Africa. It's another country and very far away."

"Do we have to go?" I pleaded with tears in my eyes. "This is absolutely the worse! Not much can top this."

"Look, if it's something everyone is dead set against doing I won't accept the position. But I want all of you to know, I will be refusing something I've worked very hard for. I want to do this and it's only one year. A year goes by quickly." With that said, we finished eating in silence. No one felt like talking. Not me, not Mom, not Dad—no one except Mei.

Chapter Three
Gottcha Day

"Here she comes—the girl of the day," Mom announced as Mei raced into the room and slid across the kitchen floor. Dad and I sat at the table while Mom finished making French toast. She always makes French toast on special occasions.

"Happy Gottcha Day!" we called out. I felt miserable after Dad's announcement yesterday at dinner, but I knew I couldn't spoil Mei's special day. So I decided not to think about moving to South Africa until tomorrow. If I don't think about it, maybe it will go away.

Gottcha Day was the anniversary of when we flew to China to pick up Mei. Some adopting families celebrated their Gottcha Day on the day they brought their child home. Others considered it to be the day the adoption became final. It didn't matter. There was no wrong day to celebrate.

Mei sat down at the table and pulled on my dad's sleeve. "Daddy, tell me again how I got adopted?"

"Mei, you heard that story a dozen times," I said. I tried not to be grouchy, but really.

Dad ignored my comment. "Sure, we were in our room in Chengdu when we received the news the nurses had arrived at the hotel with the babies. Everyone had to go to the guide's room. What was his name, Kathy?"

"John."

"That's right...John. Do you remember, Shelly?"

"Yeah, I remember wondering which baby was Mei."

"So how did you find out?" Mei asked.

"We went eenie, meeney, miney, mo."

Mei turned to Mom and said, "Mommy, was that how?"

Mom smiled and answered, "No, certainly not. Stop teasing your sister, Shelly! John called our name and the nurse handed you over to me."

"What did I do?" Mei asked.

"You just kind of stared at us," I said. "I didn't know what to say to you. I remember being really nervous about the whole thing, but then you reached out and grabbed my finger. I have to admit, I'll always remember how you did that, Mei. I think that was the exact moment we became sisters—just like that!" I said snapping my fingers.

"Did I cry?"

"No, not really," said Mom. "Shelly's right; you just stared from person to person."

"Later you cried when Mom put you in the bathtub. And boy, did you cry. I swear, the whole hotel heard you."

"I did?" giggled Mei. "Why did I cry over that?"

"You weren't used to baths," Dad answered. "I guess in China the nurses washed you with a cloth or sponge." Mei smiled as she always did whenever we talked about her Gottcha Day. She loved hearing about it.

"So what do you want to do?" Mom asked Mei. "This is your special day. You get to choose."

"Yeah, pick something good," I said trying not to be too bored.

"Can we go to an IMAX movie? I love those."

"It's yours," Dad said pointing his finger at Mei. "Let's see what's playing." Dad picked up the phone and called the theatre about the schedule. "Okay, here's what we have. There's a show on pyramids at noon; one on elephants at 1:00; a show on underwater sea creatures at 2:00; and a program on the rainforest at 3:00. So, Mei, what do you want to see?"

"Can we see two of them?"

"Well, they're each one hour so as long as they're back to back we can. Which two do you want to see?"

"Elephants and underwater sea creatures," Mei hollered as she clapped her hands together.

"Okay, that means we have to be there by one o'clock," Dad warned.

"Great choice of an activity, Mei," I said. Since I was a little kid I always liked IMAX. It wasn't a typical movie. You sat in chairs that seemed to go straight up. The huge screen put you right in the middle of the action. Sometimes I closed my eyes to keep from getting dizzy.

After breakfast Mom got Mei's Lifebook out for us to look at. Adopting families often put this memory book together while they waited for the okay to fly to China to pick up their child. Mei sat on the couch with the book in her lap. She went from page to page looking carefully at each picture. We did this on every Gottcha Day...all part of the ritual.

"What's going on here?" Mei asked.

"That's the surprise baby shower Mrs. Baker threw for Mom," I said. Mrs. Baker was our next door neighbor and Mom's best friend.

"Look, there's the stuffed bear I have on my bed."

I glanced at the picture and said, "Yup, it was one of your gifts. You received a ton of presents that day."

Mei turned the page and pointed to the photo of her room. "Hey, my room looks different."

"It used to be Dad's office before it became your bedroom," Mom said. "Did you know Shelly chose the purple color for your bedroom?"

"I love purple, Shelly. Look, here's my bedroom after you fixed it up; except I don't have the crib anymore."

"Yeah, the crib's gone but the balloons are still painted on the wall," I pointed out. "You know, I did that."

"Ah huh, Mommy told me you did." Mei turned the page and pointed to the next photo. "What's going on here?"

Dad looked at the picture and said, "Oh, that. We were sightseeing in Beijing. Our guide took us around the city. That's Tiananmen Square."

"What do you do there?" Mei asked putting the book back on her lap.

"It's this large open area in front of the Forbidden City. Normally it's jammed with people, but not so bad in November," answered Dad.

"Why is the city forbidden?" Mei asked.

"That's where the emperor lived," Dad said. "He was like the king. For over 500 years no commoner could pass through those gates."

"I remember hearing about that," I said. "Mei, we walked through the gate and saw this wide open courtyard that led to another gate. We passed through that second gate only to find another courtyard. Dad, do you remember the number of gates?"

"I believe six."

"Yeah, six," I said.

"I remember the wind. It was the kind that blew dirt in your eyes," added Mom as she squinted. "That's miserable for contact lens wearers."

Mei continued turning the pages until she came to the panda bears. "Pandas!"

"That's the Panda Sanctuary in Chengdu," Mom said.

"Was I there?" Mei asked.

"Ah huh," I said, "I took those pictures with my camera. That's you in the stroller."

"The pandas look so cute."

"Ya know, I remember John told us pandas ate 40 pounds of bamboo everyday." I grabbed the blanket off the back of the couch and wrapped it around me. "And ya wanna hear something really weird, Mei? The panda's body uses only eight of those pounds. The rest becomes waste."

"Waste?" Mei asked looking confused.

"Yeah," I answered, "ya know, poop."

"Oh! Yuck!" Mei said as we all laughed.

"Shelly, how do you remember those details?" Mom asked.

"I don't know. I just thought…hmmm…a lot of bamboo and an awful lot of poop!" Mei continued to laugh so hard she almost fell off the couch.

"You two are unreal," Mom said shaking her head.

"Look guys, here's a fancy place." Mei pointed to a photo of a hotel.

Dad looked over and said, "That's the White Swan Hotel.

It's in Guangzhou. People who adopt a baby in China usually go to Guangzhou to get their official papers signed."

"Did we do that?" Mei asked.

"Yup, otherwise we would not have been able to get you into the United States. Many adopting families stay at this hotel. They call it the baby hotel."

"Was the White Swan the only hotel there?" Mei asked.

Mom said, "No, but this place was next door to the American Consulate which was where we had to go to get your papers signed."

I looked over Mei's shoulder to get a better look at the hotel. "That hotel had this large rock in the hotel lobby with a Chinese pavilion on top. See? There's a picture of it."

"Don't forget the gardens and fountains," Mom added.

"Was I there?" asked Mei.

"Yes, you were," answered Dad. Mei took a deep breath and smiled.

Mei turned to the last page that showed friends and family greeting us after we arrived at the airport. "Here's Grandma and Grandpa with Uncle Charlie holding a sign."

"They were so excited to see you, Mei," said Mom as she pushed back a stray piece of hair from Mei's eyes. "They wanted to welcome you into our family."

"Well, I hate to break this up," interrupted Dad as he glanced at his watch, "but time is getting away from us. We better get dressed and head for the theatre."

Mei jumped off the couch and yelled, "Yeah, let's get this Gottcha Day started!"

Chapter Four
Breaking the News

"South Africa!" Erin gasped as we sat down for lunch in the cafeteria.

"You're moving to South Africa?" Katie added. "No way! Shelly, that's so far. Why are you going there?"

"This really stinks," cried Amy. "After you told me last night, I couldn't think about anything else."

"You can't stop thinking about it? What about me? I'm the one who's going. Moving to another town is bad enough, but all the way to South Africa?" Katie, Erin, and Amy were my closest friends. Actually, I didn't meet Katie until sixth grade when her family moved here from Boston. I liked her immediately. She sat behind me in Mrs. Jeffries homeroom. We started talking and before I knew it, I had made a new friend. It's not always easy connecting with people in a forever way but we did that day. I found it either happened or it didn't.

"So, Shelly, what's taking you there?" Katie asked biting into her hamburger.

"My dad's taking a sabbatical from teaching. He's using it to do research at some college there."

"Why does he want to do that?" Erin asked.

"Something about a fantastic experience," I groaned. "It might be fantastic for him, but not for me."

"Does your mom want to go?" Katie asked.

"No, but she's starting to go along with it. She says it's only for a year. We won't be selling our house; just closing it up."

"Oh, a year—so you're not moving there forever?" Erin asked.

"Erin, a year *is* forever!" I said as I took a bite out of my sandwich and then slapped it down onto the tray.

"Hey, I remember when I first heard we were moving from Boston. I hated the idea of leaving my friends, my neighborhood, and all the stuff I was in. But then when I got here, I met you guys. Soon I found I was able to do the same things here that I did in Boston. Actually, it didn't turn out as bad as I had imagined."

"Katie, you didn't move to the other side of the world. I won't even be able to call any of you!" I felt a huge lump growing in my throat as I vocalized those words. Bad enough having these thoughts float around in my head, but even worse to say them.

Amy looked at me with hope in her eyes. "You know, your mom may be right. A year does go by fast. Look! It's November already. Doesn't it seem like we just finished ninth grade?"

"I know. But I'll be away for my junior year. I'm going to be so out of it when I return."

Erin said, "No you won't, Shelly. Everyone likes you. We'll be here waiting for you."

"Do they have internet there—in South Africa?" Katie asked.

"They must. My dad emails the people at the university."

"Well, there you have it," Katie pointed out. "We can email and tell you what's going on."

"That's right," said Erin, "all the juicy gossip—who's going out, who broke up, what we're wearing to the dance."

"So you see, you won't be entirely out of it," reassured Katie.

"I guess," I said staring down at my half-eaten sandwich.

"What about Mei?" asked Amy. "Is she happy about the move?"

"Oh, she doesn't understand how far South Africa is. At first she thought we were going to China!" Everyone laughed upon hearing that.

"Where in South Africa will you be living?"

"What do you mean, Amy?"

"Like…will you be in the bush country?"

"Bush country? I don't think so. My dad said we'll be living in Cape Town. It's actually a city in the southern part of Africa, next to the ocean."

"Sweet," said Amy. "You're going to be close to the beach. It's going to be like a vacation."

"Which ocean?" Katie asked. "South Africa's next to two of them."

"The Indian Ocean is right there but I think we'll be closer to the Atlantic."

"Probably like Florida," Amy added. "You know, with

the Atlantic on one side and the Gulf of Mexico on the other."

"Yeah, whatever. Anyway, I did a search on Cape Town. I guess it's somewhat of a tourist destination."

"Tourist destination?" asked Erin. "Hey, that means there'll be things to do."

"Like what?" I wondered aloud.

"I don't know—museums, shops, places to eat," Erin suggested as she shrugged her shoulders, "all the stuff tourists do."

Amy nodded her head in agreement. "The Cape of Good Hope is there, too. Remember the explorer unit in fourth grade? Who was that dude that sailed around South Africa—was it Vasco da Gama?"

"Yeah, he's the one," said Katie.

"So what was the big deal about him?" asked Erin.

"I think there were a lot of thieves taking stuff from people who were traveling to Europe from India. Da Gama was the guy who found a way around Africa by water so these people could keep from getting robbed. Don't ask me how I remember that," said Katie, "it just popped into my head."

"Like you are so brilliant," teased Amy.

"You never know when you'll need some of that information we learn in school," Katie said slapping her palm on the table."

"Yeah...whatever," I said feeling a little agitated over this conversation.

"Shelly, I just thought of something!" interrupted Amy. "Will you be going on any safaris? I always thought that would be a cool thing to do." Amy enjoyed an adventure. Too bad her dad wasn't the one going to South Africa.

"Safaris? I don't know. I hadn't thought about going on

any safaris. Hmmm…that could be fun. I wonder how you get to do that."

Katie laughed and said, "Park your car, pay at the booth, and stand in line."

"You're thinking of Disney World," ribbed Erin.

"*Could* be fun?" Amy cried. "Shelly, it's the real deal! You can't be in Africa and not go on a safari. Wow, you're so lucky. First, you get to go to China to pick up Mei. Now you're going to live in South Africa for a whole year. That's really cool. The more I think about it, the cooler it gets. Why aren't you happy about it? We'll be stuck here at Jackson High doing the same old crummy stuff."

"I really wish you guys were going, too."

"Shelly, do you remember what you said to me on the bus four years ago?" asked Amy.

"Four years ago? I've said so much on the bus. How can I remember from four years ago?"

"Well, I do." Amy reached across the table and touched my arm. "Right after we realized we'd be in different classes at Bradley Middle School, you said it didn't matter because our friendship would last."

I smiled as I recalled that day. "Yeah, I do remember saying that. Hey, look! The friendship did survive!"

"That's my point," said Amy. "It did and we'll still be best friends when you return." With that, Amy put her hand out and gave me a high five. Then Erin and Katie reached out and gave me their high fives.

"We *will* survive!" we all agreed. It's so important to have a best friend. How lucky I am to have three.

Chapter Five
The Audition

"I do entreat your grace to pardon me
I know not by what power I am made bold,
Now how it may concern my modesty,
In such a presence here to plead my thoughts;
But I beseech your grace that I may know
The worst that may befall me in this case,
If I refuse to wed Demetrius."

"**O**kay Shelly, very good," said Mrs. Lopez. "Tell me why you want the part of Hermia and why I should choose you?"

"I think Hermia's part is cool. I'd hate it if my father forced me to marry someone I didn't like. Plus the part could be a real challenge and I love challenges."

"This part also comes with a huge commitment—lots of lines to learn and rehearsals. Are there any after school activities that could interfere?" Mrs. Lopez asked as she jotted a few words on her clipboard.

"No, the only thing I have outside of school is dance. I take jazz but my lesson is early in the evening on Thursday. There won't be a problem with me staying after school for rehearsals."

"I'll keep that in mind. Thanks for trying out, Shelly. I'll have the results on the board next to the auditorium door at the end of the week."

"Thanks, Mrs. Lopez." I walked off the stage, picked up my books, and sat down in the back of the auditorium next to Natalie.

"So, what do you think?" I whispered. Natalie Avery and her family were part of our Chinese adoption support group. We met the Averys along with the Hoffmans, Presleys, and Boyds when my family went through the adoption process to get Mei. They also had adopted from China.

"You did great!" Natalie said as she patted me on the arm. Being in a play looks like fun. I'd like to try out but I can't—with basketball practice, games and all."

"Yeah, did you hear Mrs. Lopez? She wanted to know if I had any after school conflicts."

"I did hear that. You can't blame her. I know my coach hates it when we miss practice," Natalie said as her blonde pony tail swayed in agreement.

I liked Natalie; so easy to talk to—always joking.

"Do you know who else is trying out for the part?" Natalie asked.

"Molly Simpson and Kylie Brezman are. I think Kylie is going to be my biggest competitor."

"Well, she's definitely dramatic even when she's not acting," Natalie laughed.

"Check it out! I think she's auditioning next."

Kylie walked confidently up the side steps to the stage.

Natalie was right. Kylie always acted like everything was a big deal. When she laughed, everyone heard her. When she told a story, her arms waved all over the place. Kylie reached the center of the stage, placed her hand over her forehead, and in a loud voice screeched,

> *"Take comfort: he no more shall see my face;*
> *Lysander and myself will fly this place.*
> *Before the time I did Lysander see,*
> *Seem'd Athens as a paradise to me."*

"No problem here, Shelly. She stinks!" Natalie said as she chomped on her gum.

"Shh, Natalie, you're bad."

"I'm bad? Kylie's bad! You had emotion in your voice when you said your lines, but it sounded natural; not forced like with Kylie."

"Natalie, shh! People will hear you." We watched as Kylie continued to give her academy award performance until Mrs. Lopez finally stopped her.

"Thanks, Kylie. No more is necessary." Then she asked Kylie the same questions she asked me.

"We've been spared," Natalie mumbled under her breath.

"Molly, you're next!" Mrs. Lopez announced.

Molly sat several rows behind Mrs. Lopez. She had her script in her hand as she walked hesitantly up to the stage.

"Molly, do you know your lines? I rather you not use a script for the audition."

"I do," said Molly, "but I'm afraid I might forget them."

"Do the best you can." Mrs. Lopez's instructions flustered Molly. Rattled, Molly laid her script on the chair next to where she stood. She took a deep breath.

"Lysander riddles very prettily
Now much beshrew my manners and my pride,
If Hermia meant to say Lysander lied.
But gentle friend, for uh... for... uh..."

Molly struggled for the next line. I felt terrible for her.
"She's dying inside," I whispered to Natalie.

"She's also dying on the outside," quipped Natalie.

"Molly, take a moment and look at your script. I'll let
you try again." Mrs. Lopez jotted down a few notes on the
infamous clipboard.

As Molly studied her part, I saw her hands shake. Even
though she was one of my competitors, I found myself
feeling bad about her situation. A few years ago this kind
of thing would have happened to me. After a few minutes
of dead silence, she took a deep breath and tried again.

"But gentle friend, for love and courtesy
Lie further off...uh...in...uh...human modesty."

"Thanks, Molly," Mrs. Lopez interrupted. "The results will be on the board at the end of the week."

"It doesn't look good for her, Shell. Mrs. Lopez didn't
even ask her the questions she asked you and Kylie."

"Yeah, I feel sorry for her. I hope this audition doesn't
discourage her forever," I said as I looked down at my
watch. "Uh oh, let's get out of here. I have to call my
mom."

I picked up my coat and backpack and we quietly
pushed down the metal bar that opened the auditorium
door. Just when we thought we escaped, the door made
the biggest CLANG as it shut behind us. Startled, we

looked at each other, laughed, and hurried out the building. I could hear my heart beat as I pulled out my cell.

"Hi, Mom, I'm done. Can you pick me up? Oh, and can you give Natalie a lift? I guess the audition went all right. Natalie thinks I did okay."

"Mrs. Kilpatrick, she did great!" Natalie yelled into the phone.

Having a friend in my corner is the best thing. Who's going to be there next year? How will I get those needed confidence boosts when I'm on the other side of the world? Tragedy!

Chapter Six
Mitchell

"Natalie said it didn't look like my nerves were on overdrive," I explained to Amy as I sat on the floor with my back leaned up against my bed—my favorite place to sit whenever I talked on the phone. "Kylie did great but very dramatic. You know, hands waving and all. I felt so bad for Molly. She didn't know her lines and had to stop in the middle of the audition to look at them."

"Oh, that's not good," said Amy. "You know how Mrs. Lopez feels about showing up unprepared. I can hear her now, 'My time is just as valuable as yours. Don't waste it!'" Amy shrilled her best Mrs. Lopez voice.

"You're too funny. Actually, she didn't make a scene at all. She thanked Molly and told her to look for the results on the board."

"That's interesting," Amy said. "She's not that nice to me when I'm late turning in my English assignment."

"Time to eat," Mom yelled up to me.

"I better go. Dinner's on. See ya on the bus tomorrow."

"Okay, remember only four days until you find out whether you're Hermia or the prop girl."

When I got downstairs I sensed something was wrong. Mei sat on the bench in the corner of the room sobbing while my parents tried to console her.

"What's the matter?" I asked.

"I don't want to go on the bus anymore," Mei sobbed.

"Why?"

"There's this mean boy on the bus. He's always picking on me."

"Who is it?"

"Mitchell," both of my parents said together.

"Oh, him," I said.

"You know this kid?" Dad asked.

"Yeah, he's a bully. I remember him from my last year at Madison. He started out being a problem back when he was in kindergarten. I can only imagine what he's like now that he's in fifth grade. What did he do, Mei?"

"He called me names," sobbed Mei. "He says my eyes look funny and that I should go back to China."

"He said what?" I asked. "Mei, that's so rude."

Dad picked Mei up and walked her into the living room. Mom and I followed as they sat down on the couch.

"Mei, there will always be someone out there ready to pick on other kids. What Mitchell said is not true. You don't have the problem; he does," said Dad.

"What . . . do . . . you . . . mean?" sobbed Mei.

"My guess is Mitchell doesn't like himself. Maybe he feels other people are smarter than him. Or maybe he thinks he's not good in sports. Instead of trying to do something about it, he knocks down other people."

"Dad's right," I said. "There's always a reason why some people are bullies."

"Maybe," Mom added, "he's being bullied."

"No," cried Mei, "no one bullies him. Everyone's afraid of him."

"Well, you don't know that for sure," Mom pointed out.

Dad said, "He could feel like he doesn't measure up to anyone so he picks on younger kids. That makes him feel powerful and in control."

"Does he have any friends?" I asked.

"No, everyone hates him," Mei snapped.

"Well, there you go," Dad answered.

"Mei, many times kids are picked on because they don't have the cutest face, or they may have braces, or they may be overweight," Mom said.

"Yeah, some kids picked on me in seventh grade because I didn't play sports."

"They did, Shelly?" Mei asked.

"Uh huh, and sometimes kids will be mean to other kids because they don't have the nicest clothes. It's not right but it happens."

"But Mitchell said I'm . . . I'm adopted."

"So what?" answered Mom. "That's nothing to be ashamed of. You know, we could have chosen any kid in the whole wide world but we picked you. That makes you very special."

"It does?" Mei asked.

"You bet," Dad said.

"That's right, Mei. Look at me! No choice here—Mom and Dad were stuck with me like chewing gum in hair."

After Mei thought about what we told her she asked, "Daddy, why was I adopted?"

"Well, in China many people are poor. It's possible hard times fell upon your birth mother. You know, raising a child is a big responsibility. Taking care of a baby may have been something your birth mother wasn't able to do."

"That's right, Mei. She loved you and wanted to make sure you'd have a better life than what she could give," Mom added.

"So we were the lucky family chosen," I said.

"I'm glad I'm part of this family," Mei announced with a big smile.

Dad patted her shoulder. "We're glad you're part of this family, too. Hey, what do you say we get something to eat before the food gets cold?"

"Okay," Mei answered hopping off the couch in her usual manner.

"Mei," Mom said as she grabbed her hand. "I'm glad you told us about this. Always let us know whenever there's a problem. That's what we're here for."

Later that night, I heard my parents quietly talking about making an appointment to talk to Mei's teacher about the situation. After this visit, maybe Mitchell will be more selective over whom he decides to bully.

Chapter Seven
The Announcement

"Shelly, Shelly, wait up!"

I turned around and saw Erin racing down the hallway toward me. "What's up?" I asked as she caught up to me half out of breath.

"Shelly, Mrs. Lopez posted the play parts and you're Hermia."

"I am? I can't believe it!" I yelled as we both jumped up and down. "Erin, everyone's looking at us like we're crazy."

"Who cares?" laughed Erin. "This is so cool...you getting to be Hermia. I'm very happy for you."

"Thanks, Erin. I need something to be happy about. I've been nothing but bummed out since I found I was moving. Oh, look at the time. I better get to chemistry. I'll check out the board after class."

"OK, see you later," Erin called over her shoulder.

"Thanks for telling me."

Class seemed to drag on forever. Forty minutes later, I stood with Natalie in front of the board reading off who got which part.

Theseus	Robbie Benton
Hippolyta	Molly Simpson
Egeus	Patrick Dempsey
Hermia	Michelle Kilpatrick

"There you are!" pointed Natalie. "Michelle Kilpatrick is Hermia...Ta da!"

"That's me all right—Hermia," I laughed. "Can you believe it? This is so cool, Natalie. Let's check out who else is in the play."

Helena	Carla Peterson
Demetrius	Tim Hartley
Puck	Ben Malinsky
Titania	Kylie Brezman

"Look! Kylie is Titania. She's not going to like that."

"I'm sure Kylie will take the part and make it into leading lady status," Natalie said under her breath.

"Don't be nasty," I warned.

"Well, it's true and you know it."

"Not saying anything—nada," I replied as I continued reading through the names.

"Whatever!" said Natalie, "but you know it is."

Oberon	Mark Scales
Nick Bottom	Mike Raleigh
Lysander	Jeff Rickerson

"Jeff Rickerson! Oh no! Not Jeffrey Rickerson—not as Lysander!" I groaned as I lost interest in the rest of the names. "Mrs. Lopez made a huge mistake."

"What's the problem with Jeff Rickerson?" Natalie asked. "I know he's a dork, but why does it bother you he's in the play?"

"I've been in school with Jeffrey Rickerson since kindergarten. He can really get on my nerves. He's never interested in something; he's obsessed," I explained.

"And the point is?"

"Natalie, you don't understand. You haven't been in class with him like I have. In second grade, dinosaurs had Jeff forever spouting off facts about Tyrannosaurus Rex. In third grade, rocks replaced dinosaurs. Jeffrey walked around with a pocketful, and continuously dragged them out explaining the difference between a metamorphic and an igneous rock. In fifth grade, lords, castles and medieval history dominated the scene. How I hated sitting next to him in class that year."

"I understand what you're saying," Natalie said. "Last year baseball trivia ruled with Jeff knowing all the players' RBIs."

"And this year? This year it's magic. I can't be in the same room without him shoving a deck of cards in front of my face, saying, 'Shelly, pick a card.' Oh, this is the worse!"

"But I still don't get it, Shell. So what if he's in the play?"

"Natalie, he's Lysander. I'm together with Lysander throughout the play. He's the guy I'm supposed to be madly in love with."

"Oh," Natalie said looking away from me.

"Natalie, are you laughing?"

"No, I'm . . . ha, ha . . . I'm not."

"Yes, you are! This is not funny. This is a disaster. Natalie, you ARE laughing."

"No, Shelly . . . ha, ha, ha . . . okay, I can't help it . . . you and Jeff Rickerson! Wait until I tell Amy and Erin . . . ha, ha."

"Stop laughing, Natalie." Just then I sensed Kylie Brezman standing behind me reading the announcement board.

"So, Shelly, you got the role of Hermia. Congratulations," Kylie said in a flat voice.

"Thanks, Kylie. It's quite a surprise. Congratulations on getting Titania."

"Yeah, whatever . . . I didn't even try out for that part. I don't even know who she is in the play," Kylie mumbled under her breath.

"Oh, Titania is the Queen of the Fairies," I told her.

"Terrific," Kylie said in a sarcastic voice. "Oh, what's going on here?" Kylie pointed to Jeff's name on the board. "Jeff Rickerson is Lysander? Well, have fun with that!" Kylie winked at Natalie as she turned and walked away in a huff. I wanted to run after Kylie and punch her. Instead, I simply suggested to Natalie we go to lunch.

As we walked to the cafeteria, Natalie asked, "What are you thinking about?"

"I don't know. Things are just up and down for me lately. First, I'm told I'm moving all the way to South Africa and that I'll be missing my junior year. I'm going to be far from all of you guys. I'll probably be a total loner in that place with nothing to do and nowhere to go."

"I know you, Shell. You'll make friends there. Wait and see."

"Humph, then something good happens—I get the lead

part in the play. But no, things can't stay good for me. That would be asking for a lot. What do I find out? A guy that really bugs me gets the role of my boyfriend. I can't believe it!"

At the cafeteria, we grabbed our lunch and walked over to our table. Katie and Amy were already seated. Natalie wasted no time telling the girls I got the part.

"Congratulations, Hermia!" squealed Amy. "Shell, that's awesome. I'm so happy for you. You'll be sooo popular."

As Amy continued giving out her praise, I noticed Natalie secretly signaling her to stop talking.

"Why do you keep doing that, Natalie?" Amy finally asked.

I broke in and said, "She's trying to tell you to be quiet because I'm not exactly thrilled about all of this."

"You're not?" asked Katie. "I thought that's the part you wanted."

Natalie looked at me and then turned to Katie and Amy. "In the play Hermia has a boyfriend. His name is Lysander and Hermia wants to marry him."

"Cool," answered Katie. "Who's playing Lysander?"

Natalie and I looked at each other. Finally, I took a deep breath and said, "Jeff Rickerson." And with that news, my very best friends broke into laughter.

Chapter Eight
Acceptance

Dear Diary,

The past two weeks? CRAZY! We're moving to South Africa for a whole year. Can you believe I'm going to miss my junior year? I'll probably be stuck in some school with kids I'll have absolutely nothing in common with. I don't know much about the place. My dad said Cape Town is a great city and people speak English there. Amy thinks it's cool I'm going to South Africa, but she always thinks everything other people do is cool. Amy just doesn't like what she's doing.

Then I tried out for a lead role in a play and I got it. Sure, you're thinking, now I should be happy. Well, you'd think, wouldn't ya? Huh! Actually, things seemed good until I found out this kid who drives me crazy plays the lead part opposite me. What rotten luck is that! We start rehearsals after Christmas and

I'm dreading it. This Jeff guy actually came up to me the other day and told me he's happy I'm Hermia! YUCK! My life is absolutely the pits right now. Oh, did I mention Jeffrey is my boyfriend in the play? The school NERD! The kids at school are going to make wicked fun of me when they see this play. My life is forever ruined! Maybe I should back out and tell Mrs. Lopez I can't be in the play. Yeah, that's what I'll do. I'll tell her something came up and I'm going to be busy after school. I need to think about this. My head's going to explode.

Oh, and then this creepy kid has been teasing Mei—making fun of her. How mean is that! Just because Mei looks different doesn't mean anything. So what if she's adopted from China! Being mean to someone who is different is really...

Knock Knock

I jumped up and quickly hid the journal under my pillow. "Yeah?"

"Shelly, can I come in?"

It was Mom. I didn't feel like talking to anyone so I said, "Not now."

"Shelly, you haven't been yourself all week. Let's talk about it."

"I don't want to." I buried my head in the pillow. "Please go away," I pleaded from the other side of the door.

"You aren't the only one who's concerned about moving. I have problems with it, too," Mom said.

"You do? I thought you were okay with the move."

"Can I come in so we can talk?" Mom asked.

"I suppose," I groaned.

The door slowly opened. Mom walked in and sat next to me on the bed.

"Whatcha doin'?" Mom asked.

"Nothing…just thinking…I guess."

"About going away next year?"

"Yeah, I don't see why I have to go."

"Now Shelly, what would you do here all alone?"

"I could stay with Grandma or Aunt Carol."

"Well, if you did that, you would still be going to a different school. Aunt Carol and Grandma don't live in the same area of town as we do."

"Oh." I hadn't thought about that. "Maybe I could stay with Amy."

"Shelly, you're not going to stay with anyone. A year's too long for you to be somewhere other than with us. Besides, we'd miss you."

"I didn't think you'd go along with it," I answered feeling pretty defeated.

Mom stood up and looked out the window at the street below. "Before you know it, we'll be home with lots of stories about what we've seen and experienced." She looked over at me but could see I wasn't impressed by the *things to see and do* pitch. "At first I disliked going," she continued. "I'm still not crazy about it. You know, it's not only you leaving your friends and activities. I'm going to miss Aunt Carol, Grandma and Grandpa. I won't be seeing Mrs. Baker or any of my other friends. They'll find someone to take my place at bridge and then when I return, there'll probably no longer be a spot for me. So, you see, you aren't the only one affected by this move."

"I have an idea!" I said suddenly. "Why can't Dad go and we stay here?"

"Shelly, that's not going to happen," Mom said firmly.

"Why did Dad have to sign up for this thing? Why doesn't he just stick around here for his sabbatical and write his book?"

"I know what you're saying. But Dad's worked hard at his job and now has an opportunity to research some very important issues. Global warming affects everyone. His work can have an influence on the lives of millions of people. Not everyone gets invited to be part of such a prestigious research team. If you really stop and think about it, Dad sacrificed a lot for all of us. Maybe we should go along with his plan. It means a lot to him."

I picked up Miguel, the stuffed armadillo I've had forever, and hugged him to my chest. Other stuffed animals had come and gone but not Miguel. His place remained on my bed.

"Do you remember when we went to the beach?" Mom asked.

"The beach?" I moaned. "What does that have to do with South Africa?"

Ignoring my comment Mom continued, "Think about what happens when you swim in the rough ocean. If you go against the waves, they toss you around—right? You lose your balance, take in salt water, and have a frustrating time battling your way to shore."

"Yeah, but I don't get what that has to do with me," I whined hugging Miguel even harder.

"Just stay with me on this," Mom suggested. "So what's the best way to swim in the ocean?"

"I guess relax and just ride the waves."

"That's right. When we try to buck something we really have no control over, all we get is a rough ride. So why not relax, enjoy the experience, and let the waves carry you in."

One thing about my mom, she talks in circles but at the end there's usually some stupid message. Once more the sneaky spider trapped me in her ensnarling web.

"If you let yourself enjoy South Africa and all it has to offer," she continued, "you might discover you'll have a fun year."

"But what about school?" I asked.

"Dad's checking both private and government schools now. Don't worry, Shelly, where you and Mei go to school will be a top priority with us."

I looked down at Miguel and asked, "Do I have to leave Miguel here?" At that moment I no longer felt like 15, but more like 5—very vulnerable and anxious.

"Leave Miguel here? No way, he comes with us," Mom answered. "Oh, I have another surprise for you."

"Great! I can't take any more surprises." I buried my head in my pillow.

Mom laughed. "No, I think you're going to like this one. Grandma, Grandpa, Aunt Carol, Uncle Charlie, and Stephanie plan to visit us in Cape Town next Christmas."

"Is that for real?" I asked.

"They're seriously considering it. I told them I'm sure we can squeeze five extra people in. So what do you think about that?"

"That's sweet." I couldn't keep from smiling even though I tried very hard. Stephanie's my cousin. She's only a year older than me so not only are we cousins, we're also friends. Steph loves fish. Oh, not to eat but to have as pets. She has this huge fish tank ever! What's really weird is she named each of them like you would a dog or cat. Popeye, Hudson, and Columbus are her three favorites. Fish all look alike to me but not to Stephanie. She says they actually have personalities.

Mom said, "Yup, I feel that by next December we'll know our way around and can play tour guide." My mother got up from the bed and started toward the door.

"Mom?"

"Yeah?"

"Thanks."

"I know this is hard on you, Shelly. Let's see how it plays out. It might surprise you."

"Yeah maybe, but it's scary not knowing anything about where we'll be living. Oh, by the way, whatever happened to that Mitchell kid? Did you and Dad talk to the school?"

"We did," Mom said. "We met with Mei's teacher, the principal and Mitchell. I don't think he'll change all too soon, but I'm confident he'll think twice before he bullies Mei again."

"Why did you go to the school instead of his parents?"

"Well, a couple of reasons, Shelly. Mitchell's bullying took place at school so that should be the first place we go."

"But shouldn't you also talk to Mitchell's parents?" I asked.

"Not right away. We don't know what the situation is at his home. For all we know, he could be the target of physical abuse from his parents. Very often that type of behavior is mimicked by the child. He may feel powerless at home so bullying is how he may deal with it."

"Really?" I asked. "Do you think Mitchell is getting picked on at home?"

"We don't know but we certainly don't want to make

things worse for him. The school has been alerted and they'll handle it. I think Mitchell was surprised to see us confront him at school. Mei said she will tell us if he bothers her again."

"Is the school doing anything so Mitchell doesn't pick on other kids?"

"The school psychologist will talk to him and evaluate what to do next."

"That's good. You know, it really fries me. Who cares if Mei's adopted from another country; so what if she looks different. She's still Mei."

"I know," agreed Mom. "Some kids think everyone has to look like them, talk like them, wear the same kind of clothes, and act the same way. And if they don't, well—they're unacceptable. Fortunately, growing up usually takes care of that type of thinking."

"What do you mean?"

"Often when kids get out of high school and go to college or to work, they begin to recognize how much more interesting it is if the bowl has apples, oranges, and bananas in it; not just apples."

"Mom, you can be so weird at times," I laughed.

After Mom left, I slipped off the bed and looked out the window. The weather report called for an early snow storm but it hadn't happened yet. It sure would be great if we had a snow day tomorrow. I could use a day off with nothing to do but be lazy. I decided to wear my white socks to bed that night. Amy swears by that. Wear white socks and a snow day will happen. Remembering my journal, I returned to my bed and retrieved if from its hiding place under the pillow.

"Let's see, Miguel, where did I leave off? OMG, I don't

know why I talk to you as though you can understand me. You're only a stuffed animal."

In the play, Jeffrey is my boyfriend. The school NERD! The kids at school will make wicked fun of me when they see this play. My life is forever ruined! Maybe I should back out and tell Mrs. Lopez I can no longer be in the play. Yeah, that's what I'll do. I'll tell her something came up and I'm going to be busy after school.

I immediately stopped reading and stared at my words:

The school NERD! The kids at school will make wicked fun of me . . .

OMG...could it be true? Suddenly I noticed the similarity between my reaction to Jeffrey and Mitchell's treatment of Mei. I didn't insult Jeff to his face, but I gossiped about him behind his back. Jeffrey marched to a different drummer and my behavior reflected my intolerance. All of us kids make fun of him. Did he know? As a young boy, had he ever cried to his parents? I felt ashamed. How could I be mad at Mitchell for making Mei feel so unimportant when here I am doing the same thing to Jeff? I knew what I needed to do, and it had to be done immediately.

Chapter Nine
Decorating the Tree

I pulled the hardened clay bell out of the box and hung it onto the Christmas tree. A photo of me at seven had been glued onto it. "I remember making this in school," I said straightening it on the branch.

Mom smiled. "I always like decorating the tree. Every ornament carries a special memory from a different time."

"I like this one, Mom," Mei said as she picked up a shiny ball with a panda.

"That one is cute, Mei. We bought it while in Beijing."

Mei nodded her head. "There are so many pretty colors in it."

"Yes," Mom agreed. "Someone painted all those individual sections. Shelly, do you remember when we went to a factory to see how that was done?"

"Yeah, what's it called again?" I asked.

"Cloisonné," Dad answered.

"Yeah, that's it. Cloisonné."

"How do they make it?" Mei asked.

"It's pretty clever," Dad said. "First, they have a base. It could be a vase, a piece of jewelry, or an ornament. Then someone welds small curly strips of wire on it forming patterns or pictures."

"I remember that," I said. "Mei, these ladies paint each little section using eye droppers."

"Eye droppers? Not brushes? How does it get so shiny?" Mei asked.

"After the paint dries, they temper it by first heating and then cooling it," Mom explained.

"What does temper mean?" asked Mei.

"That means to make it stronger. They heat it up in a kiln which is like an oven. Then they cool it in cold water," explained Dad.

"Can we go back to China?" Mei asked.

"Would you like to do that?" Dad asked.

"I don't want to stay there. I just want to see it. I don't remember it at all."

"Maybe we can go back when you're a little older," said Mom. "It's very far away, you know."

"Could we go when we're in Africa?" Mei suggested.

Dad laughed and said, "I don't think that'll be a good time. Going to China will be its own separate trip. Mom's right. When you're older, like Shelly, we'll think about going. By then you'll be old enough to understand and remember what it is you're seeing."

"Do you think I'll remember Africa?" Mei asked.

"I think so. We'll be there long enough so you should remember it," Mom said handing a crystal snowman over to me.

"All we need now is the angel at the top of the tree," Dad announced. "Mei, it's a tradition that the youngest person in the family places the angel on the top."

"Yeah, it used to be my job," I said. "Now it's yours, Mei."

Mom watched Dad pick Mei up so she could reach the top branch. "I don't think your father can pick you up anymore, Shelly. He'd break his back."

"Someday Daddy won't be able to pick me up either," Mei said.

"That's when we drag a chair over for you to stand on," Dad said.

I sat down on the couch to admire our work. To me, decorating the tree marked the beginning of the Christmas season. "I can't believe we won't be here for Christmas next year."

"Do people have Christmas in South Africa?" asked Mei.

"It depends on their religious beliefs," Mom answered, "just like in America. Some celebrate Christmas while others don't."

"Don't they celebrate Kwanzaa?" I asked.

Dad shook his head. "Not in Africa, Shelly. Kwanzaa is an African -American celebration. From what I know, it's not at all a religious celebration."

"What kind of a celebration is it?" I asked.

"Kwanzaa is the time African-American people celebrate their ancestors and their culture," Dad explained.

"Do they have a tree?" Mei asked.

Dad laughed and said, "No, not for Kwanzaa. They do have a Kinara which is a candle holder and Mishumaa saba."

"What's that?" I asked.

"The mishumaa saba consists of seven candles. One is black, three are red, and three are green," explained Dad.

"Oh, like the menorah."

"Not at all, the menorah is something totally different."

"I know the menorah is part of the Jewish celebration of Hanukkah," I said. "Amy's family has one sitting on their dining room table."

"With Kwanzaa, people celebrate togetherness for the family and the community," Dad said. "They remember the past and plan for the future to see how to better the community."

"That's good for all of us to do," Mom added.

"Kwanzaa is a rather new holiday," Dad said. "This guy named Maulana Karenga started it in 1966. He felt African-Americans needed to have an event that would bring them back to their African roots."

"Mei, you're thinking about something. What's on your mind?" Mom asked.

"I hope Santa can find me next Christmas." Hearing that, we started laughing.

"What's so funny?" Mei yelled. "How is Santa going to know where I am?"

"Tell you what," I said walking over to her, "next Thanksgiving we'll write him a letter telling him we moved."

"How will we know if he got the letter?" Mei asked.

"I have the North Pole address," I answered. "Sending the letter around Thanksgiving should be enough time to let him know we're living in South Africa." I could tell by Mei's expression that she hadn't completely bought into my plan.

"Okay, I think we're done," Mom announced. "Shelly, go turn off the lights so we can get the full effect of the tree."

I walked over to the lamp and turned it off just as Dad switched on the tree lights. The tree glowed as it sent its silent message throughout the room—a message of peace, love, and hope. Mom would often say if you have those three things, you have a lot.

I looked out the window and saw the snow falling. "It looks like a Christmas card."

"It does," Mom and Dad said together as the mantle clock struck eight bells.

"Hey, look at the time. Mei, you should start thinking about bed," warned Mom. "You know, tomorrow is school. Shelly, is your homework done?"

"Most of it," I answered. "I just need to finish my math assignment." I went to my room, pulled my math book out of my backpack, and spread everything across my bed. After I finished the first geometric proof, I spotted my journal under the pillow. I hadn't written in it since last Thursday. I opened the journal and stared at the last entry—the page about Jeffrey Rickerson. I found it interesting to read something I wrote several days ago because feelings often change from one moment to the next. No longer focused on math, I picked up my pen and wrote:

Dear Diary,

It felt good to laugh tonight. I mean not a hee hee, but a big, wide-open laugh. It's been several weeks since I felt happy inside. My talk with Mom helped me feel better about leaving for a year. Don't get me wrong. I'm not tipping over with joy here. If Dad said they called the move off, I would be so on top. But I'm not totally depressed as before. Besides, I'm still here with seven whole months before we have to leave. Why waste time worrying?

On Friday I found a way to be nice to Jeffrey.

That was not easy; Jeff being Jeff. I walked up to him and told him if he ever wanted to practice his lines in study hall, to let me know. I also congratulated him on getting the part. He just stared at me with this weird look on his face. Shudder!

*Finally he said, "Okay, Shelly, we can do that."
I knew I did something good. No one had to tell me. I felt it in the middle of my brain and the pit of my stomach. You know, it felt good being nice to a dorky person. I'll have to try it again. Maybe that will make up for all the rotten stuff I've said about him.*

"Shelly," called Mom. "Natalie's on the phone. She says it's urgent!"

"Hi, Natalie. What's up?"

"Shelly, can you talk?"

"Yeah, for a little while. Why? What's going on?"

"Shelly, have you heard the latest rumor?"

"No, what?" I asked anticipating some juicy gossip.

"Are you sitting down?"

"Natalie, just tell me."

"Jeff Rickerson is telling everybody the two of you are going out."

"We are WHAT? Are you serious?" I yelled into the phone.

"He's telling people you asked him out?"

"I did NOT! You've got to be kidding! All I said was we could practice our lines together in study hall."

"Well, that's not how he took it, Shell. What are you gonna do?"

"I don't know. I can't believe that jerk's telling people

that. My life is ruined! Natalie, you have to tell everyone none of that is true."

"I've been doing that," answered Natalie. "I think that Kylie girl is part of the problem. I think she's been spreading the rumor to whoever will listen. Look, I gotta go. My dad wants to use the phone. I just wanted to warn you."

"What am I going to do, Natalie?"

"Don't worry, Shelly. This will get straightened out. We'll talk in school tomorrow, okay? Bye."

"I can't believe what is happening!" I yelled into my pillow.

"Shelly, what's the problem?" Mom asked as she opened the door to my room.

"Problem? No problem, Mom. Everything is absolutely fantastic!" I answered in my best sarcastic voice. "Please, just close the door. I want to be alone."

"Okay, but it sounds like something is wrong," Mom answered as she backed out of the room.

Feeling crummy, I opened my journal only to see the words I had just written jump out at me:

Maybe that makes up for all the rotten stuff I said about him.

"Scratch that!" I mumbled as I scribbled out that last sentence.

Natalie just called and told me everyone thinks I'm going out with Jeff! I can't believe it. For one second I'm nice to that idiot and then he starts telling everybody we're going out. How can I show up at

school tomorrow? How can I face people? OMG...
This is totally embarrassing. I know...ride the wave!
But it's a big one.

Chapter Ten
First Rehearsal

The second day back from Christmas vacation found us in the auditorium. Mrs. Lopez handed out the script and the rehearsal schedule. After going over the dos and don'ts, she pointed out the pages we needed to memorize by next week.

"Okay, people," (Mrs. Lopez always calls us people), "it's important that everyone having lines on the first ten pages have them learned by Friday. In order to be ready for the show in March, it'll be necessary for everyone to stick to the schedule. Right now, go through the script and highlight your parts."

As we highlighted, I peeked over and saw Jeff sitting at the opposite side of the auditorium. I purposely walked in after him to make sure we sat far apart. This whole situation stressed me out. I announced to the world I wasn't his girlfriend. I even told Amy and Natalie to tell Jeffrey's best friend, Karl, that in no way did I consider Jeffrey as my boy-friend, and that he better stop telling everyone we're going out. That seemed to work or so I hoped.

"Okay people," said Mrs. Lopez, "the first scene takes place at the home of Hermia and her father, Egeus. We have Egeus telling Hermia that she's to marry Demetrius. She tells her father that she doesn't love him. She loves Lysander instead."

Was it my imagination or did the girls sitting behind me laugh when they heard Mrs. Lopez say that Hermia loved Lysander? Not a loud laugh; more like a muffled, inside joke laugh.

"So," Mrs. Lopez continued, "let's have Egeus and Hermia come to the table to read their lines." As I walked up front, I could hear the whispers. I turned around and saw Kylie Brezman poking the girls around her.

Later that evening, I called Amy and told her what happened. "Amy, when I heard the laughter, I looked over and saw it came from where Kylie sat."

"That's just like her," Amy said. "You know, she's jealous you have the part she wants. Don't let her get to you."

"But it makes me want to quit the play."

"That's the last thing you should be thinking!" Amy scolded. "That's what Kylie wants you to do so she could have Hermia's role. Think about it, Shelly, this is psychological warfare."

"Do you think Kylie would be that mean?" I asked.

"Oh yeah, she's used to getting her way. Not getting that part is killing her. Just act like you don't care and she'll give up her little game," Amy advised.

"Okay, I'll try, but it's not going to be easy."

"Is Jeff still thinking you're his girlfriend?" Amy asked.

"No, I think he got over that after you and Natalie talked to Karl."

"Shelly, come on down and set the table," Mom called.

"Amy, I better go. My mom's calling me."

"Yeah, I have to go, too. See you at school tomorrow, and don't worry. Bye."

I went downstairs and found my dad showing my mom some tickets. "What's that?" I asked.

"Oh, a little surprise for you and Mei," Dad said as he winked across the room.

"Not another surprise," I groaned. "I'm beginning to hate surprises. Tell me. What is it?"

"Go get Mei and we'll tell both of you girls at dinner," Mom said.

I found Mei in the living room drawing pictures of butterflies in her sketch pad. She could do that for hours. Mei not only enjoyed art, but she was very good at it. When we went to the open house at her school, it surprised us to see how her art work topped everyone else's in the class.

"Mei, we're eating now and Dad has some kind of a surprise for us." I didn't have to say another word. Once Mei heard me say "surprise," she dropped her crayons, jumped off the couch, and ran into the kitchen.

"What's the surprise?" Mei asked as she slid into her chair at the table.

"Well girls, we're going to New York City for a few days," Dad announced.

"New York City?" I yelled. "YES! When?"

"Where's New York City?" Mei asked.

"It's about 200 miles from us," Mom explained.

"I've always wanted to go to New York," I said. "When are we going?"

"Well, once both of you calm down, we'll fill you in on

the details," Dad teased as he reached for the salad dressing.

"Early in February," Mom answered. "Dad's going to New York to meet with some people about the research project in South Africa, so we thought all of us could tag along."

"We're taking a train into the city on Thursday evening after school lets out, and we'll be staying until late Sunday afternoon. I have to meet with a couple of people on Friday. I'm sure the three of you can find something to do while I'm busy."

"That's awesome," I said twirling spaghetti on my fork. "What are the tickets for? Ya know, the tickets you were showing Mom when I walked into the kitchen."

"You certainly don't miss a trick, do you Shelly? You should be an investigative reporter when you get older. Do you think we should tell them now or keep it a secret?" Dad jokingly asked Mom.

"Tell us now. Remember, I hate surprises."

"Okay. We discovered the Chinese New Year falls during the time we're in the city. So we bought tickets to see the Chinese New Year show at Radio City Music Hall."

"Oh, this is just too cool—Radio City!"

"What's a Radio City?" Mei asked. We all laughed once we realized Mei had no idea what we're all excited about.

"Mei, Radio City is a big theatre in New York," answered Mom. "People go there from all over the world to see entertainment. It happens that while we're in New York, the Chinese New Year show will be playing. So we have tickets to go see it on Saturday night."

"What's Chinese New Year, Mommy?" Mei asked while slurping a strand of spaghetti making it wiggle into her mouth with great speed.

"Mei, don't eat the spaghetti that way," Mom warned. "It isn't polite." Mei giggled as the sauce-covered pasta smacked her in the face.

Dad shook his head and said, "Mei, Chinese New Year is a celebration of the year to come. You see, no matter what the old year was like, this day gives a fresh start."

"Why don't they have it on the same day as us?"

"For the Chinese, the New Year celebration starts with a new moon. They don't celebrate it for one day," Mom said. "It goes on for fifteen."

"Why fifteen?" I asked.

"Because their New Year ends on a full moon and that's 15 days later."

"I never knew that. Can you pass a napkin over here?" I asked.

"A new moon and a full moon?" Mei asked. "I thought we only had one moon."

The three of us laughed. It was hysterical how little kids interpreted what they heard.

"What's so funny, guys?"

"We're sorry, Mei. We sometimes forget there are things you haven't learned yet," Mom answered. "The new moon is when the moon is not visible to us on earth. The side that's lit up is facing the sun and away from Earth so we can't see it."

"And," Dad continued, "a full moon is the opposite. The moon is completely illuminated by sunlight."

"Mei, it's the same moon, but it's in a different spot in the sky so we see it differently." I turned to Dad and asked, "So Chinese New Year starts when the moon is dark and is over when the moon is all lit up?"

"There you go," answered Dad.

"Do they celebrate all during that time?" I asked.

"Yes, each day during the New Year has a special meaning," Dad said. "Like the first day, people don't eat meat because they feel if they did, that will result in a short and unhappy life. On the second day, they pray to their ancestors."

"Shelly, could you clear the table while I put the dishes in the dishwasher?" Mom asked.

"Sure. Dad, tell us more about this."

"Here's something interesting," Dad continued. "On the second day everyone is nice to their dogs because they believe that day is the birthday of all dogs."

"No way, you're making this up," Mei said shaking her head back and forth.

"No. I'm not. That's what happens."

"For real?" Mei looked at each of us to see if we were buying it.

"For real," Dad said.

"What happens on the third day, Daddy?" Mei asked twisting her black hair around her finger.

"Well, the third and fourth days are when the husband pays respect to his wife's parents. You see, in China the daughter lives with her husband's family. So a special visit is made to her family."

"That's cool," I said becoming more interested in this conversation.

"The fifth day is called Po Woo," Dad said.

"Po Woo?" Mei and I said together.

"That's so funny! Po Woo," echoed Mei.

"Well, the words sound funny because it's in a different language," Dad said. "Po Woo is a very serious day. No one goes anywhere. They stay home to welcome the god of wealth. They feel if they go anywhere it will bring them bad luck."

"I remember when I was in sixth grade I learned the Chinese were superstitious. Did you know they avoid the number four?"

"I did," Dad said. "You know why?"

"No," both Mei and I said together.

"In Chinese, the word for four sounds similar to the Chinese word for death."

"That's why they avoid it?" Mom asked.

"Really, I never knew that," I said.

Mei anxiously tugged on dad's sleeve. "Daddy, what do the Chinese people do on the next day?"

"Well, on the sixth thru the tenth day, they visit people and pray for good fortune and health."

"A lot of Chinese tradition is about that—good fortune and health," said Mom.

"Keep going, Daddy. What happens next?"

"On the seventh day of the New Year the farmers display their vegetables, meat, or fish for everyone to see. This day is considered to be the birthday of humans. They eat raw fish for success and noodles for a long life."

"The humans have a birthday just like the dogs," Mei yelled out.

"You're right, Mei," said Dad. "This day is more important than everyone's individual birthday. Everyone adds a year to their age on that day instead of their actual birth date."

"That's kind of weird," I said. "What goes on during the eighth day?"

"They have a family dinner and pray to Tian Gong," Dad answered.

"Who's that?" I asked.

"He's the god of Heaven."

Mom turned the dishwasher on and joined us at the table. "I can see the women of the house do a lot of cooking during those two weeks."

"And everyone else does a lot of eating," I added. "What goes on the ninth day?"

"That's the Jade Emperor's day when people make an offering to him," Dad explained, "and then friends and relatives are invited for dinner on days ten thru twelve." We laughed as we looked at Mom. She shook her head from side to side.

"More cooking," she moaned.

"And more eating," I added as I looked around at everyone.

"Ah, but then we have day thirteen," Dad said. "That's when you eat rice and mustard greens to cleanse the digestive system."

"Naah, not true," I said. Dad had a habit of teasing and we never knew if this was one of those times.

"Not a joke, what I'm telling you is right. I read up on this."

"What goes on during day fourteen?" Mom asked. "Does the mom of the house get to stay in bed and rest?"

"Of course not," Dad answered. "She must get ready for the Lantern festival that's held on the 15th night."

"More cooking!" Mei yelled out.

"So what's this Lantern Festival?" I asked.

"On the last day of the New Year celebration people carry lanterns into the street for a big parade," Dad said. "We hope to get down to New York's Chinatown to see this parade. It starts at one o'clock on the day we leave. I think we can see some of it before catching our train home."

"Are the kids out of school that whole time?" I asked.

"No," Dad answered. "In the United States all these celebrations are shortened. The stores in Chinatown don't close for two weeks, and Chinese Americans don't take off from work that whole time. So it's made simpler. Much of what I mentioned is arranged in the evenings or on weekends so everyone's daily schedule isn't affected."

"Like other customs brought from Europe and other places of the world, they're modified," Mom explained.

I stood up and announced, "Modified? Shouldn't the word be Americanized? And speaking of Americanized... uh, is there any dessert?"

Chapter Eleven
New York, New York

"Look at all the taxi cabs!" Mei yelled pointing to the yellow cars that whizzed by while we waited for the traffic light to change.

"There must be hundreds of cabs in this city," Mom said. "Lots of people live and work here and many of them need transportation."

"Don't they have their own cars?" Mei asked.

"Having a car in New York City can be a problem because of traffic and parking," said Dad.

I looked across the street and saw steam blasting from vents in the pavement. Many of the roads were one way streets with the traffic going only in one direction. The light hadn't changed, but that didn't keep the herd of people from crossing as they dodged a swarm of honking cars. Once on Fifth Avenue, I looked up and spotted the marquis above Radio City Music Hall announcing the Chinese New Year Show.

"I've never been in such a large theatre before," I said walking from the lobby down to our seats. A woman looked at our tickets and pointed us in the right direction. I turned around and saw three rows of balconies above us.

Mei looked up and said, "It's like we're in a yellow cocoon."

"You're right. Actually, the ceiling looks as though it could fold like a paper fan." As we sat down, I noticed several people standing by the stage holding signs that said *No Cameras Allowed*. Watching the people file into their seats fascinated me. I wondered if they lived in the city or traveled from some distant place.

Soon the lights went down, the music started and the program began. We watched a variety of acts—singers, dancers, musicians. A man and a woman introduced each act by explaining the meaning behind the performance.

"What do you think about all this?" I asked Mei during the intermission.

"I like it a lot, especially the dancers." I could tell. Her eyes grew huge and she didn't move from the time the first act started.

After the show we went to a small restaurant to eat dinner. The place had small tables with wrought iron chairs. On the floor lay a brown rug with pebbly swirls. Some people ate alone while others dined with friends. Next to us sat another family. They had a small boy who entertained himself by following the swirls in the rug with his toe. I found it interesting how some people kept themselves amused.

Several chefs wore tall, white hats as they stood behind the kitchen station. Each one was completely focused on the dinner orders he had to fill. Alongside the wall were buffet tables with steam coming from the covered pans. We were hungry and ready to eat.

"So everyone, what was your favorite part of the show?" Dad asked after we gave the waiter our order. "Shelly?"

"I liked the dancers especially the ones that flew across the stage holding those long, red streamers. They filled the stage with everyone going in different directions. I thought it was awesome."

"I liked the costumes," Mei said. "They had lots of shiny stuff on them."

"The costumes were beautiful, Mei," Mom agreed. "The colors were so bold—red, violet, green, yellow, lavender."

"I also liked their hats," Mei added. "Remember the ladies who had the hats with a stack of bowls on top and pearls hanging down?"

"Well, that's certainly a unique way of describing them," laughed Dad.

"What was your favorite act?" I asked Dad.

"Hmm, I have to vote for the Mongolian chopstick dancers."

"Who were they?" I asked.

"You know, the men pretending to be eagles and horses? They were pounding chopsticks against their bodies."

"Oh yeah," I said taking a sip of my water, "pretty weird stuff."

Mom shook her head and said, "Pretty different stuff, Shelly, not necessarily weird."

"Weird, different, whatever," I mumbled under my breath.

"I'll try to ignore that, Shelly. Okay, now it's my turn. I loved it when the huge stage in Radio City had nothing on it but the black grand piano. The stage backdrop showed a rugged cliff and a willow tree totally surrounded by clouds and the top of a mountain."

"Why was that your favorite?" I asked.

"I don't know; the simplicity of it all. And then that lady walked out wearing a yellow gown with white gloves up to her elbows. When she sat down at the piano, even though she looked so small on that enormous stage, she gave such a huge performance—very classy."

"What are we doing tomorrow?" I asked.

"We're taking the subway down to Chinatown to see the parade," Dad answered.

Mom added, "Sounds like a plan. But tonight let's just walk around Times Square, take in the sights and sounds, and feel the energy of the city."

Chapter Twelve
The Show Down

"So—tell me about New York," Amy said as she stood by my locker.

"We had a great time. It's really a cool city."

"What did you do?"

"Lots—we went to the top of the Empire State Building, shopped at Macy's, and saw a great Chinese show at Radio City."

"Did you go to the parade?"

"Sort of," I answered.

"Sort of? What's that mean?"

"When we got down to Chinatown it seemed like everyone else in the city had the same idea. There had to be a gazillion people all waiting to see the parade."

"It was crowded?"

"Crowded wasn't the word for it. It was mobbed. We

couldn't get anywhere near the street to see the floats and bands. At one point there were two bunches of people headed in opposite directions with me in the middle. The people crammed in front of me tried to get by in order to escape the crowd, while the people in back pushed forward to see the parade. This one guy kept saying, 'Excuse me, excuse me.' I finally asked him where he thought I should go. No fooling, Amy, it was a wonder I didn't get crushed—totally insane."

"That's too bad you never got to see the parade."

"We didn't, but Mei did."

"How did she see it?"

I pulled my math book out of the locker along with my notebook, shut the door making a metal upon metal clang, and started walking toward my fifth period class. "Mei sat on top of my dad's shoulders so she saw everything. She sent down reports to the three of us. But a lot of other cool stuff happened all around us. Every now and then you'd see two people inside a lion's head with its tail dragging behind. You know, just walking along the sidewalk."

"Any Dragons?" Amy asked.

"Absolutely, you'll always see dragons. We also heard these popping sounds."

"Firecrackers?" Amy asked.

"Supposedly, but they really weren't. Real firecrackers would be too dangerous in those crowded streets. So instead they had these cardboard cylinders. When you twisted the top end, it POPPED! Then all of this colored confetti shot up in the air and floated down—quite awesome. A lot of that went on."

"Amy, Shelly! Wait up!" I turned around and saw Katie racing toward us.

"Hey, what's happening?" I asked.

"Are you going to your rehearsal after school today?" Katie asked.

"I plan on it. Why?"

"Well, Lindsey Malinowski told me that Kylie plans to do something to make you look bad in front of Mrs. Lopez."

"Her again—what's she up to now?"

"I don't know. Just be aware, Shelly. She can be nasty," warned Katie.

"I know. So can I if I have to be. Oh, there's the bell. We better get to class. Thanks for the heads up, Katie."

The rest of the afternoon sped by and soon I stood behind the curtain waiting for my cue to go on stage. Kylie walked by and gave me one of her sickening, black widow spider smiles that only Kylie could give. I quickly looked away, not wanting to get into it with her. After all, what could she do? We put the play on in two weeks. Everyone had a pretty good handle on their lines and entrances. We just needed to make everything run smoother.

"Okay people," Mrs. Lopez bellowed from the other side of the curtain. "Time is wasting. Let's get this performance moving. Hermia, Egeus, Demetrius, and Theseus—you're first on stage. Take it from the top—Act One, Scene One."

I immediately took my place on the stage between Patrick Dempsey who played Egeus, and Tim Hartley who was Demetrius, the guy my father wanted me to marry.

"Where's the king—Theseus where are you?" Mrs. Lopez yelled out.

"Right here," answered Robbie Benton.

"Okay, let's start with Hermia's line."

"I do entreat your grace to pardon me
I know not by what power . . ."

Once I finished my lines, I went backstage, sat down on a metal folding chair, and opened my script to follow along.

"How's it going?" bellowed a voice from behind that startled me. I turned around and saw it was Kylie.

"Good," I answered looking back at my script.

"I heard you went to New York over the weekend," Kylie continued.

"Yeah, we did."

"I went there last summer. Did you go to the Statue of Liberty?" she asked.

"No, but we saw it from a distance—too cold to go over," I answered becoming a little suspicious as to why she acted so friendly. Inside my head I could hear Katie's voice saying, "Kylie wants to make you look bad in front of Mrs. Lopez." I didn't see how this conversation about New York could harm anything. Before I knew it, Kylie sat down next to me and began to explain in detail how they rode this boat over to the Statue of Liberty. On and on she rambled about the size of the statue and the many stairs they climbed to reach the lookout level. I listened politely as I tried to keep up with the action on the other side of the curtain, but Kylie's gabbing in my ear made this difficult.

"HERMIA! WHERE ARE YOU?" Mrs. Lopez yelled. "Shelly, why aren't you on time for your entrance?"

Flustered, I immediately stood up and raced onto the stage. "Here I am, Mrs. Lopez!"

"Your entrance is on the other side of the stage, Shelly!" Mrs. Lopez pointed out.

"Oh yeah—I'm sorry." I ran to the other side while

everyone on stage waited patiently. "Where are we?" I whispered to Jeff.

"You're supposed to tell me to find a spot to sleep."

"Oh, okay . . . thanks!"

"Shelly, come to the front of the stage, please," Mrs. Lopez yelled out in an irritated voice.

"I'm sorry, Mrs. Lopez."

"What's going on backstage? Are you sleeping?"

"No, I was distracted," I nervously answered as everyone watched.

"Distracted?" Mrs. Lopez responded. "There's no time for distraction, Shelly. We have a show to give in two weeks. There's a lot to be done between now and then. I need everyone to pay attention whether they're on stage or off. That means everyone –even Hermia."

"I know, Mrs. Lopez. It won't happen again."

"Good. Now continue."

I took my place in the center of a cluster of trees that represented the woods and faced Lysander.

"Be it so, Lysander: find you out a bed;
For I upon this bank will rest my head..."

When I finished my lines, I left the stage and saw Kylie sporting the same black widow spider smile she wore on her face earlier. Immediately Katie's words, *"Just be aware, Shelly...she can be nasty,"* popped in my head.

I fell for it. Kylie started that conversation about New York on purpose. That was no accident; so obvious to me now. Well, she succeeded this time, but it won't happen again. What a snake!

Chapter Thirteen
Meeting Up With Friends

"It's been awhile since we saw everyone," Mom said as we piled into the car to join our Chinese adoption support group. "The Boyds are expecting us in fifteen minutes. Too bad we're all so busy. I miss not seeing these people." Mom turned to me and asked if the salad was in the car.

"Right here," I said pointing to the bowl on the seat next to me. "I see Natalie all the time at school." Dad backed the car out of the driveway, and we headed down our quiet street towards the highway.

"That's nice," Mom answered. "We missed the last get together because of New York. Mrs. Presley told me they had a good time."

"Lily said they celebrated Chinese New Years by eating Chinese food and popping firecrackers," Mei said waving her arms in the air. Lily Preston came over from China as a two year old; about a year after Mei came to live with us. The girls always paired up and caused mischief whenever they were together. Whichever part of the house they occupied, you could expect some commotion. Soon Dad parked our car in front of the Boyd's brick ranch.

"Hi Dave," Dad called out as we walked into their home. I liked Mr. Boyd. He always had a funny story to tell.

"Hey Steve, Kathy, girls—come on in. Everyone's here. How was your trip to New York?" Mr. Boyd asked.

"We had a great time," Mom answered. "New York in the winter was actually not bad. There's so much energy in that city."

At that moment, Mrs. Hoffman walked into the room. I once overheard my mom tell Dad that she listened well and every group needed someone like that.

"We've never been to New York," Mrs. Hoffman said as she hugged my mom, "and here it's only a few hours away. Now that Thomas is doing so well, we'll have to make the effort to take the kids."

Six-year-old Thomas was the Hoffman's adopted son. Boys rarely were available for adoption in China, but because Thomas had several health issues including a cleft pallet, exceptions were made by the Chinese government. It seemed he would get something corrected and then he would be back at the doctor's office to fix another problem. After years of speech therapy, little evidence existed that he once had a hole in the roof of his mouth. Thomas was a year older than Mei, but because of his health problems, they were both in kindergarten.

Suddenly, Natalie Avery popped into the room. "Hey Shelly, Chelsea and I are in the basement. Come on down."

Eager to escape all this adult conversation, I took my

cue and left. I found the girls sitting on the couch watching a movie on TV.

"What's happening?" I asked.

"Nothing much," said Chelsea. "We're just sitting here watching this movie." Chelsea Boyd didn't go to the same school as Natalie and me. She went to West Side High School, our school's rival. Natalie and I teased Chelsea when Jackson High won the football game against West Side last fall. She pointed out that West Side came out on top the previous three years. But it's what happened this year that mattered, or so we told her.

Chelsea not only had an adopted sister named Kim but also a brother, Jon, who was not adopted. "Jon got his junior driver's license and he's forever thinking of excuses to take the car out. You wouldn't believe how often he needs to go to the library." We all laughed over that one. "My mom won't allow him to drive with any kids in the car—not even me."

"Would you want to go with him?" I asked.

"That's a good question," said Chelsea. "It might be cool to drive to the mall without any adults, but I don't know if I'd trust my life to my weird brother."

"Watch this part, guys," Natalie interrupted pointing to the TV. "This guy's hiding behind the door and will jump out just as it closes."

"How do you know that?" I asked.

"Saw the movie six times!" Natalie said. "I have the DVD at home."

"Six times? You're kidding!" Chelsea laughed.

Somehow I couldn't get into the movie. I pretended to watch, but instead I kept thinking about this support group. Having so much in common, we've become close friends.

"Shelly, I thought you were so good in the play."

"Thanks, Chels."

"We tried to find you afterwards, but there was such a mob backstage."

"Yeah, everyone's family and friends were crowded in the hallway."

"Chelsea's right. You guys did a fantastic job," said Natalie. "I even understood what was going on."

"I have a question," said Chelsea. "Just something I wondered about. What's with the girl who played Titania?"

"Titania?" I asked.

"Yeah, the Queen of the Fairies."

"Why do you ask that?"

"No reason—she looked like she had an attitude. Was Titania supposed to be that way?"

"Ha! You see, Shelly," Natalie said as she slapped her hand on her leg and pointed into the air. "Chelsea doesn't even know Kylie and she came up with the attitude thing."

Confused, Chelsea asked, "So what's with this Kylie person? I take it she's not one of your BFFs."

"BFF?" I asked.

"Yeah, best friends forever," Chelsea explained.

"Oh yeah, that's for sure," I laughed. "You're talking about someone ticked off because I won the part that she wanted in the play."

"She didn't get her way!" Natalie pitched in.

"Anyway, the play was lots of fun and I made some pretty nice friends."

"Even Jeff Rickerson," Natalie laughed.

"Believe it or not, even Jeff Rickerson."

"I don't know any of these kids," Chelsea complained.

"My guess is your school has one or two Jeffs and Kylies," Natalie said. "Probably all schools have a few."

"Girls, are you down there?" Mrs. Boyd called from upstairs. "We're getting ready to eat."

"We're coming, Mom," yelled Chelsea.

Once upstairs, I picked up a plate and headed toward the food table. I helped myself to pizza and chicken wings; then sat at a small table where I overheard Dad's conversation with Mr. Hoffman, Mr. Avery, and Mr. Boyd.

"So what will you be doing over there, Steve?" asked Mr. Boyd.

"I'm going to be part of a research team dealing with some basic issues of how global warming may affect the crops and wildlife in South Africa. We'll be collecting data and using it to determine what could be done to reverse or slow down the problem."

"So global warming is a reality?" asked Mr. Boyd. "Some believe it's a hoax."

"Not at all, there's evidence that what's happening is very real," Dad answered, "and Africa is a continent that will suffer the most."

"How's that?" asked Mr. Hoffman.

"Just a two degree increase in temperature will trigger a sharp decline in the amount of crops produced on that continent. This, in turn, will result in increases of malnutrition, malaria, and other related problems."

"Just two degrees can make that much of a difference?" asked Mr. Boyd.

"Half of all deaths due to malnutrition occur in Africa," Dad answered. "It's estimated that the number of people affected by hunger could potentially increase from 30 to 200 million worldwide."

"Why so many?" asked Mr. Boyd.

"Africa and western Asia could suffer large crop losses," Dad answered. "These areas are heavily dependent upon agriculture and have little purchasing power. At the same time, if there is famine, this will often result in conflict and violence which can lead to political instability."

"I imagine in the poorer areas of Africa, millions of people could be displaced due to this lack of food and water," said Mr. Boyd.

"You're right. Even the more prosperous areas of the continent will feel the affects as large numbers of people start migrating across their borders."

"That must mean South Africa," added Mr. Hoffman.

"Yes," said Dad. "South Africa is one of the more stable African economies. But a two degree temperature change will drastically drop the water availability in southern Africa. Many farmers in this area have already noticed this in their fruit industry alone. Trees aren't getting the amount of time needed for winter resting. Plus the fruit tends to get sunburned during the ripening season."

"Is there a danger that this area could become a desert climate like in other parts of the continent?" Mr. Hoffman asked.

"There is," Dad answered putting his glass down on the table next to him. "Western storms bring rainfall to the Cape area, but this could all change. These rainstorms could move south missing much of the continent. Instead, all of that water could be dumped into the sea. The scarcity of water will bring a greater demand for human consumption leaving little for agriculture."

All other conversation stopped as everyone tuned into what my dad was saying. I saw a look of concern on their faces.

Mrs. Presley said, "Steve, has global warming already impacted South Africa?"

"It has. The last few years the Cape's wheat production decreased and this is just the beginning. Higher temperatures and the lack of water have resulted in wildfires. This can also be seen in our own country."

"But there have always been wildfires. That's nature's way of replenishing its nutrients," Mrs. Boyd argued.

"The difference, Sandy, is the fires are more powerful bringing with it more destruction."

"So what will you be doing in Cape Town?" asked Mrs. Hoffman.

"There's a self-funding organization based at the university. They're involved with research, consulting and training. I'll be working with them," Dad answered. "They've been around for about thirty years, and have already established themselves as a leader in integrated environmental management."

"How's that?" asked Mr. Avery.

"Mainly through an interdisciplinary and participatory approach," Dad explained.

"What's that mean?" I asked. Dad glanced over at me with a surprised look on his face. I guess that's because I never cared before about his work or even inquired why he would be in Cape Town. Yeah, I knew about the research thing, but that's about it. Actually, from seeing the interest of everyone in the group, I began to realize the importance of this project.

Dad smiled. "Shelly, this organization uses their research by consulting and training others in communities already experiencing some of these problems. They've started a variety of projects with the goal of reaching some solutions."

"Who do they work with?" Mr. Boyd asked.

"Government authorities, educational and environmental professionals, students, and members of communities to name a few," Dad answered.

"Wow, your dad has an awesome job, Shelly," Natalie whispered in my ear.

"Yeah...I guess so," I replied feeling a little embarrassed.

"I plan on posting our activities, so if any of you want to be placed on the list, just let me know."

"Yes, put us on," said Mr. Boyd. "We'll definitely be following along to see how this gets implemented."

Chapter Fourteen
An Unexpected Invitation

"Pssst, Shelly...here...take this...quickly!"

I looked over only to find Amy passing a note my way. We were in the middle of chemistry and Mrs. Paulson never thought highly of note passing. I slowly placed my hand behind me, and Amy slipped the small piece of paper into my palm. I closed my hand and discretely stuck the note in my folder.

Nervously, I looked over at Mrs. Paulson who was writing the definition of an ion on the board.

An ion is an atom or a molecule that has lost or gained one or more electrons giving it a positive or negative charge.

When the coast appeared clear, I looked down at Amy's hurriedly written note. What? Could Amy be right? Or was this another nasty rumor? I looked over at her and she gave me this familiar look she always gave when she wanted to tease—one eyebrow raised up while the other remained in its normal position. I never could do that—no matter how hard I tried. No longer was this lesson on ions a priority with me. Instead I turned around and looked back at the note to make sure I read it correctly.

Shelly,
  The word going around is that Josh Zettleman is going to ask you to the Junior Prom. Is that cool or what? You better tell me the minute he does.

Amy

Oh wow! Josh Zettleman asking me to the prom? That can't be right. He's one of the most popular guys in the junior class, the quarterback of the football team, and the top runner in track. He's asking me?

Finally, the bell rang. I scrambled up my books and immediately headed over to Amy. "Amy, that can't be true. Josh has never even talked to me. Besides, he goes out with Caroline Fenster."

"Not anymore," Amy replied. "Erin told me that Cindy Whitman told her they got into a huge fight and broke up. So he's going to be asking you to the prom. You are so lucky. You're going to need a dress. I'll help you pick one out."

"Wait a minute. He hasn't asked me yet. Besides, he doesn't even know I exist," I argued.

"Well, he saw you in the play and thought you were cute. So now that he needs a date to the prom, he's asking you."

"Are you serious? Oh Amy, something popped into my

head. I don't know if my parents will go along with this. My mom thinks you should only go to the Junior Prom if you're a junior. They're so weird that way."

"Shelly, you'll be sixteen in June. Bring that up. Tell them you won't be here for *your* Junior Prom because you'll be stuck out in Africa somewhere. Play the guilt card. It usually works."

"Yeah, I could do that."

"Hey, there are more important issues here. What will you wear?"

"Wear? I don't know. I'm not going to think about any of this, Amy. He hasn't asked me and he may never. Rumors are just that—rumors."

"Maybe so, but I better be the first person you tell when he does. Find out if he has a friend who needs a date. I'll be happy to fill the position. That would be sooo cool, Shelly, us going to the Junior Prom together."

All morning I waited for the invitation from Josh, but nothing happened. A few times I passed him in the hall as I walked to my next class, but he gave no indication that he even noticed me. At lunch Amy and Erin relayed to Natalie what they knew. She, of course, acted thrilled. That's what makes a good friend; they're thrilled when something good happens to you, even if it hasn't.

"Shelly, there's Josh Zettleman. See—he's sitting at the popular table over in the corner and Caroline isn't sitting there. I told you, they broke up," said Amy in a hushed but excited voice.

"Amy, that doesn't mean one single thing."

"Their table is by the garbage can. Here, take this wrapper and pretend you need to toss it," suggested Erin.

"I'm not doing that. It's so obvious."

"No, it's not. Here throw my milk carton out," coaxed Natalie as she joined in on the plot.

"Go on, do it," whispered the girls as they pushed garbage into my hands.

"And walk slowly," said Amy.

"And smile," added Erin.

Before I knew it, my feet were headed over to the garbage can and the popular table. I walked very slowly and had this stupid grin on my face as I looked over at Josh. I didn't have to turn around to know the girls followed my every move. I wanted to disappear and forget this ridiculous scheme but— too late. Next thing I knew some of Josh's buddies were punching his arm and motioning over to me. Could I make myself vanish? I continued my journey towards the garbage can. It seemed like forever. Finally, I reached the can and threw milk cartons and food wrappers into it. In the corner of my eye I noticed everyone at the popular table staring at me. Everyone, that is, except Josh. His face had turned beet red. He looked everywhere but at me. Oh my gosh, could the rumor be true? The longest walk of my life finally ended with me sliding back into my chair.

"Girls, I'm like freaking out right now. I can't believe I let you talk me into doing that. I just may never speak to any of you again!" I looked at the large clock on the wall and announced, "I'm going to be late for my next class. Bye."

"See ya, prom girl," Natalie said laughing hysterically.

The rest of the day left me paranoid. Every time I heard my name, I jumped. I wondered if I would run into Josh and if so, what would I do? How would I respond? As it turned out, little cause for worry. The school day finally ended and I arrived home without a trace of an invitation.

The phone rang as I entered the house. I placed my

backpack on the chair and headed toward the kitchen to grab something to eat.

My mom called out, "Shelly, are you home?"

"Just got in."

"You have a phone call."

I walked over to her and as I took the receiver, Mom winked and whispered, "It's a boy."

Chapter Fifteen
The Junior Prom

"Shelly, tell me everything. Don't skip a thing," Amy said over the phone.

"The prom was so much fun and Josh was so cute. When he picked me up, Jake and Beth were already in the car."

"I can't believe it—you doubled with Jake and Beth? They're the coolest couple in the junior class. What were they like?" asked Amy.

"They were okay. Beth acted standoffish. You know, she and Caroline are close friends, so I'm sure it wasn't her plan to have me as part of their foursome." I stretched out on the floor and rested my feet on top of the bed.

"I can only imagine. Did you see Caroline at the prom?"

"Oh yeah, talk about weird. She and Brian Bentley arrived late. I caught a glimpse of her glaring at me—so obvious."

"What did Josh do?" Amy asked.

"Nothing, he just ignored her."

"Okay, tell me everything from beginning to end," Amy insisted.

"Well, let's see. They picked me up and my mom took pictures of the four of us. That was awkward especially since I didn't really know them that well. And Mei? I could not believe her."

"Why?"

"She hid behind the chair in the living room. I gave her a dirty look, but she remained behind the chair and giggled. I could have died right on the spot. I know Josh saw her. I felt so stupid."

"That's what little sisters do, Shelly. Now you can understand what I've been living with all these years with Gracie."

"Then there's my dad. Asking things like, when will you have her home? Are you a responsible driver? Do you have your senior driver's license?"

"You've got to be kidding!" Amy said in a horrified voice.

"I'm not kidding—so lame."

"My dad would have done the same thing, Shelly. Parents! They think we're still little kids. So what happened after you made the escape from your house?"

"We went to eat at The Cove on Thistle Lake."

"Shelly, how cool is that? That's one of the best restaurants in town and right on the lake. Was anyone else there?"

"Yeah, all the kids from the popular table."

"I think I'm going to faint!" Amy said in her most dramatic voice.

"Josh introduced me to his friends and they were nice

to me. Our food came and while we ate, everyone told stories about people they hung out with. I listened and laughed whenever they did. But I didn't feel a part of it. Matter of fact, I felt like a jerk. Then after dinner, we went to the prom."

"Any sophomores at the prom?"

"I saw our buddy, Kylie, at the dance."

"You mean our very own Titania?" Amy had this way of impersonating Kylie by using an uppity and proper voice. Having practiced it so often, Amy could nail it like no one else.

"The one and only; I have to tell you, she had on the most obnoxious dress."

"OMG! She did? What did it look like?"

"First of all, it didn't fit her well at all—too tight. It looked like she jammed herself into the dress. And the color? It wasn't a pretty emerald, but more a florescent green. She lit up the place."

"You can bet that was her intention," Amy said sarcastically. "Did Kylie talk to you?"

"Barely, but mostly gave her infamous smirk as I walked by. Kylie looked surprised to see me with Josh. She came with Marcus, the guy who keeps score at the basketball games. He's kind of cute."

"Yeah, but he's not Josh. What's more, he certainly doesn't sit at the popular table."

"Maybe not, but that doesn't matter so much to me."

"When it comes to Kylie, it should. Shelly, that's two points for you."

"I'm not competing with Kylie." I sighed. "I just want to do my own thing, but she keeps showing up."

"Hey, it couldn't have been more perfect," Amy said. "So tell me, what else happened?"

"Not a whole lot. The gym looked great. It was decorated with red and white flowers and matching streamers. At one end of the room we had our picture taken by a water fountain someone had set up for the occasion. Then we stood around and listened to the music and talked."

"Did you dance?"

"We did, but most of the time everyone talked. It would have been more fun being there with all of you guys. I can't believe I'm going to miss my own Junior Prom next year. That really stinks!"

"Yeah, I know. It's a bummer. Ya know, it stinks for me, too—you not being here and all. At least you'll be seeing new things and checking out a new place. I'm going to be so bored next year."

"But you'll have Erin, Katie and Natalie," I said trying to cheer her up a little.

"I know but it's different with us. We've done things together since we were little."

I never thought about how hard my leaving would be for Amy. We've been best friends for so long; always at each other's house or constantly on the phone. A deafening silence followed until Amy broke in with another question.

"Do you think he'll ask you out again?"

"Who?"

"Josh, you ding-a-ling."

"Oh, him—I don't know. I told him I'm leaving for South Africa in July. He thought that was pretty cool."

"Why did you tell him that?" Amy squealed over the phone.

"Why? Because I'm leaving for South Africa in July! Anyway, whatever happens, happens. It's probably good if it ends right now. I don't need to add anything more to the 'Why I Feel Crummy About Leaving' list."

"Shelly, I just thought of something. Didn't you say there will probably be kids at your school from other countries? Maybe you'll meet some dude from Italy or France? I can hear it now, 'Ah Shelly, vous inquiéteriez-vous pour partager mon déjeuner avec moi?'"

"Amy, you are so weird. I think you live in a major fantasy world. I need to go. Just don't say a word about any of this to anyone."

"Okay, but couldn't I at least tell Erin and Katie?"

"Well…okay."

"And Natalie?"

Chapter Sixteen
June

I didn't need to wonder for too long if there would be a second date with Josh. A week after the prom, word got out that Josh and Caroline were back together. It's probably just as well with me leaving town. I actually felt bad that Caroline didn't go to the prom with Josh. After all, they went together all year. Even though I had an incredible night, he should have taken Caroline.

June came upon us suddenly. We had so much to do. Trying to decide what to pack and what to leave behind posed to be a challenge. Dad advised to be selective because of shipping charges. He left for Cape Town a week ago to find a place for us to live and a school Mei and I could attend. Right now he's staying with someone named Charlie.

"So who's this Charlie person?" I asked as we piled the clothes onto the bed.

"Someone that works at the university," Mom said.

"Charlie's family invited Dad to stay with them until he locates a place for us to live."

"Are the houses in South Africa like ours?" I asked.

"Sure, Cape Town has neighborhoods. Dad will find something suitable. Try not to worry."

"I'm not worried."

"I think you are. What's going on inside your head?" Mom asked.

I looked down at the floor and started to cry. I couldn't help it. I tried to keep everything inside, but it came gushing out.

"I knew it," Mom said as she sat down on the bed and put her arm around me. "Let it out and then we can deal with it. What's bothering you?"

"I don't know. The move seemed so far away when I first heard about it and then...all of a sudden...it's now."

"Are you worried that you'll miss your friends?" Mom asked.

"No, it's not that. They all promised they'll stay in touch especially through email. My worry is not what I'm leaving behind but what I will face."

"And what are you afraid of?" Mom probed.

"Like...what kind of school will I be in? Will the kids ignore me? What if there's nothing there to do? Will I be able to keep up with my classes? How will I get to school? Will there be clubs to join? Those kinds of thoughts clutter my head. I forgot about it for awhile, but now that we'll soon be leaving, I can't. I'm really afraid, Mom. And I guess I'm not used to being afraid."

"It's scary whenever you start off in a direction that's brand new. But maybe you should look at it as a kind of adventure. Things will be different for all of us, but some things will be the same. And those different things can be a little exciting. Look at it as a time not only to learn about another country, but also another part of the world. Just think, Shelly, you won't be visiting South Africa. You'll be experiencing it and for a whole year. That's a great opportunity for all of us, don't you think?"

"When you put it that way…yeah, I guess so."

"Mom," yelled Mei from downstairs. "Dad's on the phone."

Mom looked at her watch and said, "Oh, it must be around eleven o'clock there. They're a good six hours ahead of us." I followed her as she quickly got up and ran to the phone. I wanted to know what Dad found out.

"Hi, Steve. We're fine. You did? What's it like? That sounds great."

"What's he saying?" I asked.

"Can I talk to Dad?" Mei interrupted as she pulled on Mom's sleeve.

"Not now, Mei. This phone call is expensive. Girls, Dad's found a house for us to rent. I'll tell you more later."

Mom continued to talk but I couldn't make much sense of the conversation at my end. At times Mom appeared concerned and I wondered why. I hung onto every word until she ended the conversation with, "That sounds good. The girls will be happy to hear that. Really? Sure, I'll tell them. Talk to you soon."

"What did he say?" I asked. "What sounds good?"

"Okay, here's the scoop," Mom said hanging up the phone. "Dad was able to find us a house that's furnished. It seems the people that own it are living in Johannesburg for a year so it's a perfect match."

"Do I have to share a room with Mei?" I asked.

"No, it's a three bedroom ranch style house with a small backyard. What's even better is that it's near the school you'll be attending."

"Dad found a school?" I asked.

"Uh huh, it's a government run high school that's very progressive. The principal told him that it not only has a strong academic program but also a great drama club."

"How did he find that out?" I asked unsure if it was too early to celebrate.

"He talked to the principal today and went on a tour. He liked what he saw and said that Charlie told him the school has an excellent reputation. Plus, Shelly, your concern of how you'll get there will not be an issue."

"Why's that?"

"The house is only four blocks from the school," Mom said. "But there's one little problem."

"Problem? Oh boy, here it comes."

"Nothing we can't work out; don't look so worried. It seems South Africa's seasons are opposite ours. They have winter when we have summer."

"I know about that. Why is that a problem?"

"What that means is their school term goes from January until November. Their summer vacation is for six weeks beginning in December and running some time into January."

"I don't get it."

"When we arrive, school will already be in session," Mom answered.

"How's THAT going to work? I'll be starting in the middle of their school year? Oh, this is just great!" I yelled as I threw myself on the couch.

"What's the matter?" Mei asked.

"Not much for you, Mei. It's me who's going to have a

big problem here," I said picking up a magazine and slamming it down on the coffee table.

"Shelly, stop that! Let's talk about this rationally. It's not like you're the first kid in the world who has had to move to another school in the middle of the year."

"But how am I going to do that, Mom? Half of their junior year is already over. I'm not going to enter as a sophomore. I just finished that up."

"Shelly, you don't have to. Look, you've been in advanced placement classes the past two years. The chemistry and math you took as a sophomore are normally taken in the junior year. The way I see it, you can cross those two subjects off the list. They're done. As for social studies, English and Spanish, you can pick up wherever they are."

"That's going to be hard in Spanish."

"But you'll have extra time to focus on it. We can get you a tutor for the Spanish if there's a problem."

"You make it sound so easy," I complained.

"No, we just have to be positive."

"What about me?" Mei asked.

"Mei, you're going to a primary school that's also close to the house. I'll be dropping you off and picking you up everyday. Dad said you're being enrolled in first grade. You've done a great job learning how to read in kindergarten and whatever extra help you might need, I can tutor you at home."

"Does that mean we don't get a summer vacation?" I asked.

"Well, it looks that way," Mom answered. "Hey, you'll have the first week of July off. Then you'll get the whole month of December and part of January as a vacation. That'll be cool, don't you think?"

"Oh brother," I groaned. "I get out of school and I immediately start back with no break."

"Girls, I told you there would be adjustments. This is one of them. Just go with it."

"Do we have a choice?" I asked in my best sarcastic voice.

"Not really," Mom replied as she tossed a sock at my head.

Chapter Seventeen
Sixteen Candles

"Hi Natalie, come in. Shelly and the other girls are in the living room."

"Thanks, Mrs. Kilpatrick," Natalie stumbled into the room holding a sleeping bag, a backpack, and a small package in her arms. "Are you guys all set for South Africa?"

"As ready as we'll ever be," Mom answered. "We finished the packing, and the truck arrived last Monday to pick everything up."

"So soon? You're still here for one more week."

"We have to ship it early," Mei answered twirling around in her stocking feet.

"Oh, it's going by a slow boat to China," Natalie quipped.

"China? Not China, silly…South Africa," Mei answered putting her hands on her hips.

"Don't mind Mei. Kids this age take everything literally,"

Mrs. Kilpatrick said glancing over at her daughter. "Mei, Natalie is only joking."

"No problem, Mrs. Kilpatrick. Neither did Lin get a joke at five. Sometimes she's still that way and she's nine. Where can I put all my stuff?"

"Just drop it on that chair for now," said Mom.

"Natalie, did you bring it?" Amy whispered as she rushed into the room.

"Yeah, we got it yesterday. My mom wrapped it just before I left the house. That's why I'm a little late."

"That's okay. We're all here now. I can't wait for Shelly to see what we got her."

"Hey, what's happening out there?" I called.

"Happy birthday, Shelly!" Natalie yelled. "Sorry I'm late."

"You're not late," I answered. "You're just in time."

It had been a few years since I had a birthday party with my friends, but because I'll be leaving for a year, Mom agreed to have a combined birthday/going away party. So I invited my closest friends—Amy, Erin, Katie, Natalie, Chelsea, and my cousin, Stephanie—to a slumber party.

"So girls, get your suits on if you want to go swimming," said Mom. "We'll be having dinner at about six o'clock. Mei, you come with me."

"Why can't I stay?" Mei whined as she followed her mother into the kitchen.

"Today is Shelly's time with her friends. So come help me get things ready for dinner."

We spent the rest of the afternoon lounging around the pool, reminiscing and gossiping about everything and everyone. Whenever we were hot, we'd jump in the water and cool off, trying hard not to get our hair wet. I couldn't help but think how different this party was from the one I had five years ago. "Girls, do you remember the Olympic birthday party I had when I turned eleven?"

"Yeah, I do," said Chelsea. "You had all kinds of pool games."

"Right—we used the Olympic theme because later that fall we left for China to pick up Mei."

"Weren't the Summer Olympics held in China?" asked Amy.

"Yeah, that was the connection," I said.

"Would you believe I still have the medals I won?" pitched in Amy.

"Hey, how come I wasn't at that party?" Katie asked feeling a little left out in this conversation.

"That's because we didn't like you," teased Erin while the rest of us laughed.

"That's not true, Katie. I had that party the summer we were going into the middle school. We hadn't met you yet."

"Oh, that's when I moved here from Boston," Katie said feeling a little better. "Okay, all of you are forgiven—that is, everyone except Erin."

"So Shells, what's the story? Have you heard anything from prom boy?" Stephanie asked.

"Yeah Shelly, what's up with him?" Chelsea added.

Stephanie and Chelsea went to another high school so they weren't as tuned into things as the other girls.

"Okay, let me tell you how this all unfolded," Amy said. "You see, Josh broke up with Caroline a month or so before the prom. The story circulating is that they got into this huge argument! Josh saw Shelly in the play and decided to ask her to the prom."

"Is this Josh cool?" Chelsea asked.

"Cool? He's the most popular guy in the junior class," Amy answered.

"And don't forget Jake and Beth?" Erin interrupted.

"Who's that?" asked Stephanie. Whenever Stephanie got excited her eyes doubled in size.

"Jake and Beth are the second coolest couple in the junior class—next to Josh and Caroline," Amy answered. "But at that time, Caroline was out of the picture."

"It really doesn't matter," I said shaking my head at the girls. "Josh and Caroline made up. Besides, I'm going to South Africa for a whole year so who cares anyways."

"I take it you didn't have a good time at the prom?" Chelsea asked.

"No, it was fun but awkward at times. Beth acted like a brat, but I guess she wished she was doubling with Josh and Caroline—certainly not me! Plus there seemed to be a lot of whispering behind my back. I don't know. Maybe I was paranoid, but whenever I glanced over at Caroline, she either glared at me or pretended to be having a great time with her group."

"I would have freaked out," said Natalie.

"What did Caroline do?" Erin asked. "You never told us about that."

"She'd laugh and act as though something hysterically funny happened. It was so obvious."

"Yeah, how come guys don't see through those things?" Chelsea asked.

"They're kind of dumb that way," Amy answered. At that point we started to laugh. Then Natalie got up from her seat and said she had to do something. When she returned she held a beautifully wrapped present.

"What's this?" I asked.

"This gift is from all of us," Chelsea answered. "We thought that instead of each of us giving you a present, we would pitch in and buy you something special."

"It's both a birthday and a going away present," Erin added as she sat on her towel next to my chair.

"We thought this gift would help you keep in touch with us while you're gone," Amy said.

"Now you have me guessing! I can't wait to see what it is. Thank you so much."

"Open it!" Erin and Stephanie yelled.

I slowly pulled the card off the package and read what each girl wrote.

"When did you guys do all this?" I asked.

"Behind your back," Amy laughed, "just open the present."

I ripped off the ribbon and pulled the wrapping paper away letting it fall to the ground. I held up a small box containing a digital camera inside.

"Oh, wow! A camera—this is so nice. Thank you so much."

"Your mom told us your camera was old," Amy said.

"It is but what made you think of this?"

"We wanted to get you something you could use while in South Africa," Erin explained. "Then Natalie came up with the idea of a camera. You'll have lots of things to take pictures of and share with us when you return home."

"Plus you can actually download the photos and email them," Natalie suggested.

"Yeah, if you have any friends we want to see what they look like," said Stephanie.

"What do you mean…IF I have any friends?"

"Okay, that didn't come out right. When you meet a new friend," Stephanie said. "Is that better?"

"Yes, much better. Besides, Stephanie, you'll be out there next Christmas so you can actually meet them—whoever they are!"

"Lucky you, Steph," Amy sighed. I reached over and gave Amy a big hug. I knew of all my friends it was Amy who I'll miss the most. We've spent so much time together that not having her around will be awful.

"I want a picture of an elephant," Chelsea said. "You'll be seeing elephants, I hope."

"My parents said that a safari is on the list of things we must do while there. So, yeah, I can definitely get you a picture of an elephant. Thank you so much. I love my camera. It's the best thing anyone could have given me. I'm going to miss...all of you... so much." Just as I started to choke on my words, we stood up and gave a group hug. I felt a little tap on my back, looked down and there stood Mei.

"What's going on?" she asked. She looked sweet staring up at me. Mei had no idea what it was like to be pulled away from what you're used to and then pushed into unknown territory. But then again...of all people, she does. She was a baby when she left the orphanage in China. I'm sure there'll be a time when she'll begin to wonder about that part of her life. I hope to be there for her when she does.

"Come in, Mei," I said pulling her into the circle. "I need my friends and my sister right now."

Part Two

Cape Town, South Africa

"Things don't change. You change your way of looking, that's all."

Carlos Castaneda
(1925-1998)

Chapter Eighteen
Leaving the Familiar Behind

We picked up our luggage at baggage claim and followed the other passengers through customs. Upon exiting, we saw many people lined up and waiting; several held signs showing the name of the person they planned to pick up. No sign needed for us. There stood my dad with a big grin on his face. A month had passed since he left for Africa. Mom succeeded to get everything shipped. She notified the necessary people that we would be gone for a year, and then closed up our house giving my grandparents and Mrs. Baker, our neighbor, a key. We said our goodbyes to our grandparents who tearfully drove us to the airport. It didn't matter to Grandma that she'd be seeing us in December—five months was a long time to wait. My mom recited the number of people living far from their families but that didn't help. "It's what you're used to," Grandma explained as she sat between Mei and me in the backseat of the car

Grandpa was driving. My mom sat up front and stared out the window and I knew why. She didn't want anybody to see her tears.

Once on the plane, things got better. In addition to the many meals that occupied our time, we chose our own movie or video game available to us on the backside of the seat directly in front of us. I managed to sleep a little but not a sound sleep like the one Mei had. South Africa's time zone was six hours ahead of us. If you add that to our travel time, we got on the plane on a Wednesday afternoon and walked off on a Friday morning. It took forever! But we arrived and there stood Dad.

"Daddy, Daddy," Mei cried out as she raced over to him and gave him a big hug. Dad greeted all three of us and asked how the trip went.

"Long," we said in unison.

"Well, let's get all your things into the car, and I'll take you to your new home. There you can rest up, and tomorrow we'll check out the city."

"All I want right now is a shower," I said. "I feel gross. Is there a shower there?"

"Of course, Shelly," Dad said piling our luggage into the trunk of the car.

"Daddy, where did you get this car?" Mei asked.

"I leased it for a year."

"What does lease mean?"

"It means he rented it, Mei," I explained rather impatiently. She was always asking questions and after sitting next to her on the plane for a zillion hours, I was totally out of patience...none, zip, nada!

"I think we'll need to get a second car for you, Kathy."

"What about me, Dad? I'm sixteen now. I can get my

learner's permit." Nothing but silence followed. That always signaled something bad was coming around the pike. "I AM sixteen, Dad," I repeated in case he didn't hear me the first time.

"Well, honey, in South Africa you have to be seventeen to get a learner's permit."

"What? No way! Are you sure?" I asked.

"I am—checked it out the other day. But you know, this might not be the best place to learn to drive. I promise, you can get your permit as soon as we return home."

I was tired, messy, and definitely not in a good mood after hearing that. How else will I have to adjust?

"So what's your impression of this city, Steve?" Mom asked quickly changing the subject.

"Cape Town is fantastic. I know you'll like it. In some ways it's like the states, and in other ways it's so different. What I did discover is people are friendly. You'll notice that right away."

"We'll see," I mumbled. "So when do I start school?" I asked.

"Right now we're looking at Friday. This will give you and Mei six days to get organized and somewhat adjusted to things. Then you'll have one day to see what school's about before going for an entire week."

"I can't believe I'm starting school again," I grumbled. "I just finished with all that."

"Did you tell her about December and January?" Dad asked Mom.

"She did," I quipped. "But I need a break now!"

"Shelly, I think it's good that school's in session. That'll give you an opportunity to meet other kids right away. Otherwise, you'd be sitting around the house bored, not knowing anyone." I secretly admitted to myself that he had a point there. By now we left the airport and pointed the car towards our new home.

"How come it's not that cold here?" I asked. "I thought it was supposed to be winter. It feels more like fall."

"You're right," Dad answered. "You see, the climate in Cape Town is on the moderate side. Rarely do they have the extreme hot or cold temperatures."

"Why, Daddy?" Mei asked.

"Because of where it's located, it's more like what you get along the Mediterranean Sea—mild, with rainy winters and sunny summers."

"How cold does it get?" Mom asked.

"I believe the evening temps could get down to the 40's and up to the 60's during the day."

"People here think of that as winter?" I grumbled. By now the lack of sleep had caught up to me. Nothing seemed to agree with me.

"It's probably like Florida, Shelly," Mom explained. "Except in Florida it can get pretty hot in the summer."

"December thru February is considered summer in Cape Town, but the temperature usually stays around 80 degrees. So it's all what you're used to," Dad explained as he negotiated the car onto the highway. "This is Route M3, Kathy; the road we take to get to our area."

"I don't know if I'll ever learn my way around here," Mom groaned.

Dad laughed and said, "Sure you will. I've been here four weeks and it's become familiar."

"Hey, Mom—what did you tell me? Oh yeah, the unknown can be such an adventure." She ignored my comment and continued to stare out the window.

"Where will we be living, Daddy?" Mei asked.

"In an area called Newlands. Cape Town has several sections. Bishopcourt, Claremont, and Rondebosch are the ones close to us. You'll become familiar with them."

We turned off the highway and headed down Struben Road. Soon we found ourselves driving down a street with tall shade trees that formed a protective canopy. Dad pulled into a brick driveway in front of a creamy white house with pale blue shutters on each side of the windows. Three brick steps reached up to a small landing that led to the front center door. A triangular overhang, held up by two white pillars, gave the impression of a small, covered porch. One lone tree grew in the side yard.

"Well, folks, here it is. Welcome to your new home in Cape Town, South Africa."

"I really like the street, Dad," I said as I peered out the side window. "It has a sidewalk. That's cool. We don't have that at home. This place looks friendly."

"Now would I choose an unfriendly street, Shelly?" Dad teased. "Come on, let's check it out." Curious to see what the inside of the house looked like, we quickly jumped out of the car. Suddenly, I no longer felt tired, messy, and cranky but sort of excited.

"This is kinda like an adventure," I pointed out.

"Now you're speaking my language," Dad laughed.

Inside the front door was a small living room that opened into a large kitchen with lots of windows. "I love this kitchen, Steven. It's perfect."

"I thought you would. Do you see how the table overlooks the backyard?" We glanced out the window and noticed the small yard totally enclosed by a brick wall and lots of trees for privacy. In the corner of the lot was a fairly large, brick fireplace for outdoor cooking. "Your school is in that direction, Shelly. Just go around the block, down a couple of streets, and you're there."

Secretly, I thought this was cool, but I decided to hold back the enthusiasm. After all, there were plenty of unknowns floating around out there.

"Where's my bedroom?" Mei asked as she peered from the kitchen door.

"Go down the hallway and your room is on the left. It's painted yellow—a little bit of a change from the purple you have at home," Dad said. "And Shelly, go take a look at yours. It's the blue room right across from Mei. It has lots of windows which let in the morning sun. I think you'll like it."

I immediately rushed down the hall to check out my new space. The room was smaller than the one at home but it'll work. At least I don't have to share a room with my sister. At sixteen, I needed my privacy…totally.

"This looks nice, Shelly," Mom said following me. "I think Dad's right. Check out the bay windows with the bench seat underneath. What do you think?"

"Yeah, I like it."

"If you lift up the seats under the cushions, you'll find room for extra storage," Dad said.

"Dad, do you think I could decorate the room?"

"Sure, but you're not allowed to hang posters and pictures on the walls. That was one of the stipulations the owners gave."

I reached into my backpack and pulled out Miguel, my stuffed armadillo. I walked over to the bed with the blue striped coverlet and placed him in a prominent spot at the foot of the bed. "Okay, I'm all set. What's to eat?"

Dad laughed and shook his head. "I think we can scrape something together. I did a little grocery shopping yesterday but I know it's not enough."

"I'll take inventory and later this afternoon you can show me where the store is," Mom said.

As they headed out of my room, I overheard Dad say to Mom, "She brought the armadillo all the way to South Africa?"

I turned from the window only to see Mom smile and shrug her shoulders.

"Hey, I heard that! You know, I might be sixteen but that doesn't mean Miguel gets the shaft."

Chapter Nineteen
Cape Town

"**I**f you look over to your left you'll see Table Mountain," Dad pointed out. That towering rock formation can be seen from all around Cape Town."

I lowered my head and saw a large mountain made up of rugged, bare rock that was flat on the top. "I can see why it's called Table Rock."

"There's even a cable car going to the top. The view overlooking the city is supposed to be fantastic," Dad continued as he drove our car through the city traffic.

"Can we do that someday?" I asked.

"Definitely," answered Dad. "You'll find many things to do here. Cape Town is a cosmopolitan city. It attracts a variety of artists, shopkeepers, and other business people. Look over there. Can you see another mountain peak?"

"I see it," Mei yelled. "It has a point on it."

"That's called Lion's Head."

"Can we go to the top of that, too?" I asked.

"Yeah, many climbers leave their cars along Signal Hill Road and climb the path that encircles Lion's Head," Dad answered.

"That's awesome," I said.

"Check out that wall of rock with the many peaks. That's called the Twelve Apostles. All of this makes up the rugged chain of buttresses and ravines that totally surround this city."

"It's absolutely beautiful, Steve."

"And in between this wall of rock and the Atlantic Ocean is the city of Cape Town," Dad explained.

"Where are we going next?" Mei asked.

"I'm taking you to a really neat spot called the Victoria and Alfred Waterfront, better known as the V&A," Dad answered.

"Look at all the ships," Mei cried out excitedly.

"Yeah, that's a shipyard. Shipping is a lucrative business here," Dad explained.

"This section looks a lot like Seattle," Mom said, "with all the ships, cranes and loading docks."

My parents went to Seattle for an environmental conference two years ago while we stayed with my grandparents. My mom always talked about that visit as one of the most interesting places she traveled to in the United States.

"You're right, Kathy. It does."

"What's that over there?" I asked pointing to a large tent across from the shipyard.

"That's the Zip Zap Circus School," Dad answered. "Interested in attending?"

"Not really. I didn't know there were circus schools," I said as I twisted my body to see out the back window.

"Oh, sure," Mom responded. "There's one in Florida, too."

"I can still see Table Mountain," said Mei pointing over her shoulder.

Outside my window, I spotted people running, walking, skateboarding, cycling, walking dogs--all by the ocean. It looked like a great place to hang out, and I wondered if I would ever be able to come down here with friends. That is, assuming I meet friends in this place. Dad parked the car once we were at the Waterfront. The place looked pretty awesome.

"They patterned the development of this waterfront project after San Francisco's harbor," Dad explained. "There's an aquarium, a shopping centre, restaurants, a pedestrian area, and lots of other interesting places to go."

I looked up and saw this tall, white building with many windows. In front hung a sign that said Victoria Wharf. The second level had a balcony with tables and umbrellas. To get to the entrance, we walked under palm trees that had red and white flowers planted underneath. Once inside, I noticed a variety of shops, eateries, and stalls where vendors sold their crafts. It was apparent this mall was not in the states. Giraffes were everywhere. Not the living kind, but ones made from wood. They came in three sizes—small, medium and large. Some could be placed on tables while others stood on the floor. African pottery and zebra pillows were displayed on tables next to safari hats, spears, candles, African clothing, post cards—so many things to check out. We walked a little further until we came to a stall displaying hand carved animals. Some were made of stone while others were carved from wood. I picked up the elephant and looked carefully at it.

"Hi, do you like it?" a voice asked. I turned around and

saw a lady smiling at me. She had laughing eyes and I liked her immediately.

"These are pretty cool," I said to the vendor.

"My brother carved them out of ebony. Look—the lion, elephant, buffalo, leopard, and the rhino. We call these the Big Five."

"Why are they called that?" I asked.

"Because they're the most dangerous animals to hunt," the lady with the big smile explained.

"What are you looking at, Shelly?" Dad asked as he caught up with me.

"The Big Five—aren't they the best?"

"Do you like them?" Dad asked.

"I especially like the ones made from wood."

"Well, you know, I wasn't home when you turned sixteen. Would you like them for your birthday? It'll be my present to you."

"Serious? Yeah, that would be awesome."

Dad picked up the Big Five and handed them over to the salesperson.

"I think you selected the best set," she said as she carefully wrapped each one in tissue paper. "The wooden animals will not break like the stone ones."

Outside we roamed amongst the many restaurants, boutiques selling hand painted clothing, and bistros with live music. After an hour of exploration, we decided to head back to the car.

"What's that red building, Daddy?" Mei asked.

"Oh, that's the Victorian clocktower." The red and black clock tower had gingerbread trim. On the second level I saw a row of long windows circumventing the tower. The third level sported a black wrought-iron gate that wrapped around its perimeter. A large clock, showing a time of 1:15, was at the very top.

"Check that out, Mom," I said pointing to the clock. "No wonder I'm starving; it's way past lunch."

"I know where we can pick up a barbeque sandwich," Dad answered. It's at the university cafeteria. Let's go and I'll show you where I work."

Chapter Twenty
Lesterford

Hi Amy,

How's it going? Sorry I didn't write sooner but things have been crazy here. This place isn't too bad. You're right—there's a lot to do. Kind of awesome, no fooling. There's this really neat mall that's right next to the ocean. We hung out there for part of Saturday. Then we went to see where my dad works, the University of Cape Town. Everyone here calls it UCT for short. We got to see his office, walked around campus, and ate lunch in the cafeteria. Next to the cafeteria is this building with all these steps leading down to a grassy area. In front is a statue of some guy named Cecil Rhodes. Don't quite know anything about this dude but there he sat with his head in his hand. The statue overlooks several rugby fields which is a popular sport here. The campus is pretty cool—old buildings covered with ivy. There are lots of walking paths with Table Mountain towering in the background. It seems like no matter where you are in Cape Town, you can see Table Mountain.

I start school this morning—school in July? That really bums me out. My mom and I went to meet Mr. Barratt, the principal, yesterday; actually he's called the headmaster here. The school I'm going to is Lesterford Secondary. The grades go from fifth to twelfth and I'll be halfway through the eleventh when I start. Because I already took chemistry and 11th grade Math in tenth grade, I won't have to take them again. Instead I'll concentrate on catching up with 11th grade History and level 4 Spanish. I'll also be taking some cool electives to finish off the year. Everyone has to sign up for a winter activity. I chose drama. I'm really psyched about that.

School here ends in late November which is weird. Then I start 12th grade later in January and get to start it again in September with you guys. My schedule will be really messed up by the time I return, but I decided no sense stressing over that until I have to. Hey, ya notice anything? I'm turning into a new Shelly! Well, maybe. TTYL

"Shelly, are you ready for breakfast?"

"I'm coming." I hit the SEND button, logged off the computer, grabbed my backpack and headed into the kitchen.

"I'm really not hungry, Mom. My stomach is doing somersaults."

"Are you nervous?"

"Uh, yes! I wish I didn't have to go. Why can't I wait and start on Monday?"

"Shelly, no matter when you start, there will be a first day so let's get it over. You'll be fine. Don't worry. Hey, you look cute in that uniform."

"No way! I look so weird. Why does everyone have to wear these?"

"That's just the way it is, Shelly. It's their policy."

"Humph...so when do you get your car?"

"Not until next Thursday," Mom answered. "Until then I'm driving Dad to work and picking him up. I have the route all worked out. As long as I don't leave the highway, I'm fine."

It didn't take long to get to the school. Actually, I could walk but Mom drove me because it was the first day. I arrived at the office and Mr. Barratt greeted us.

"Welcome to Lesterford, Shelly. I've arranged for one of the students in your class to take you around and get you started. Matter of fact, here she is now."

The glass door opened and in walked a girl dressed the same as me. Her blonde hair was pulled back with a maroon hair band that matched the sweater of her uniform.

"Hi, Mr. Barratt," said the pretty blonde-haired girl.

"Laura, come and meet Shelly. She's the girl from America I told you about."

"Hi, Shelly, how long have you been in Cape Town?"

"I got here six days ago. Thanks so much for helping me out like this. I'm feeling rather lost right about now."

"No problem, just stick with me and I'll show you around."

Laura's contagious smile put me at ease. I said good-bye

to my mom and followed Laura to history, our first class. The teacher, Mrs. Van Wyk, greeted me at the door. I took the desk behind Laura as two dozen pairs of curious eyes stared at me. I looked straight ahead stealing a side glance every so often to get a sense of who sat in the seats around me. Mrs. Van Wyk handed me a fairly large book and directed me to open it somewhere in the middle. I checked out the number of pages the class had already covered and wondered if I would be responsible for the earlier work. There I go worrying again. Just ride the wave.

At lunch I walked into the cafeteria and sat with Laura and three of her friends—Kim, Hannah and Lacey.

"Shelly, how long will you be here?" asked Hannah.

"A year—my dad's working at UCT until next July. Have you always lived in Cape Town?" I asked the girls trying to think of stuff we could talk about.

"I moved here from Holland when I was seven," said Laura. "And Hannah arrived from Ireland when she was in fifth grade." I looked over at Hannah. I couldn't help but notice her fiery red hair and the freckles that covered her face like confetti. I love freckles but people who have them usually don't.

"Kim and I have always lived here," said Lacey. Lacey was quite pretty with her creamy brown skin and black hair cut very close to her head. She also had this huge smile. As for Kim, she was tall. I think I must come to her earlobes. Not much time went by before I learned she put her height to an advantage by playing volleyball.

"Are any of you involved with the drama club?" I asked.

"That would be me," said Laura. "Soon we'll be having auditions for the musical, *Les Miserables*."

"You're doing a musical? Never did that before," I said, "but it's something I would like to try. I sang in the chorus back at my old school."

"Each grade has a play. The play put on by the junior class is specifically given to raise money for the Matric Ball," explained Hannah.

"Is that like the prom?" I asked.

"Prom?" asked Laura. "Yeah, I think so. It's held in May of our senior year. Do you think you might like to be in the play?"

"Sure, that sounds great."

"Okay, I'll keep you posted on the audition schedule."

"Hey, Shelly, we're popping into Woolies on Saturday. Think you might like to come?" asked Kim.

"Popping into Woolies? What's that?" I asked.

"Woolies is a short name for Woolworth. It's a department store in the mall," explained Laura.

"Oh, I get it now…popping into means stopping into. I don't know; I need to check with my family. I'm not sure what we're doing."

"My mom can swing by and pick you up," said Kim. "Here, let me give you my number and you can let me know if you can come."

As Kim and I exchanged phone numbers, a girl walked over to the table and stared at me. "Who are you?" she asked with a voice to freeze over water.

"Trudy, this is Shelly Kilpatrick. She just moved her from America. I'm showing her around school," said Laura.

"You happen to be sitting in my seat."

"Trudy, just sit over there," Hannah said as she pointed to an empty chair at the end of the table.

In an instant, all the comfort and confidence that started to build up inside me began to dissipate. I didn't quite know what to do. So instead I cowered and said, "Oh, I'm sorry. I can move over there." As soon as I said it, I wished I hadn't. After all, who does this Trudy person think she is—the queen of the table?

"Shelly, that's silly. Stay where you are," said Laura. "Trudy, chill out and sit over there."

All through lunch I could feel the tempo changing. The girls continued to be friendly and included me in their plans for Saturday. I ignored Trudy's cold stare and smiled as though I noticed nothing. As we got up to leave, Kim said, "Remember Shelly, let me know if you're able to join us."

"I will," I said as we left the cafeteria. Laura led me to my Spanish class. I wanted to ask her about Trudy, but decided against that. After all, I didn't know where Trudy stood in this relationship. With me being the new girl, I didn't want to cause waves. I really liked these girls and wanted them to like me, too.

"Spanish is in Room 35 B," Laura said. At the door stood a woman with a black braid twisted around her head. "Senora, this is a new student from America— Shelly Kilpatrick. Shelly, this is Senora Perez."

"Buenos dias, Senorita Shelly. Welcome to our school. I'll get you a book but for now, please take the empty seat by the window."

"I'm down the hall at math so I'll pick you up after class. We can go to the gym together," suggested Laura.

I nodded and took my designated seat as Senora Perez proceeded to introduce me to the others. When I turned around to say hi, I recognized a few of the faces from my previous classes. As I scanned the room, my eyes fell upon her. Oh, brother! I couldn't believe it. Trudy was in my Level 4 Spanish class. How lucky was that!

Chapter Twenty-One
The Mall

"Come in, Kim," I said as she and her mom stood at the door. My parents planned to spend Saturday doing errands—food shopping and getting things needed for the new house. They were happy I met new friends so quickly and actually encouraged me to go to the mall with them. My parents introduced themselves to Mrs. Broodryk and Kim. Not much time went by before we learned they lived only two streets away. My dad said he would be happy to pick us up at 4:00. We gave our good-byes and soon after we were at the Claremont Shopping Mall.

"Bye girls, have a lekker day," called out Mrs. Broodryk as we headed toward the mall entrance.

"What did your mom say?" I asked Kim.

"She said for us to have a lekker day."

"What's a lekker day?" I asked.

"That means to have a nice day," Kim explained. "I guess

every country has their slang. Do you have another way of saying that in America?"

I thought about it for a while and then said, "We might say have a good one."

"I like that—have a good one!" laughed Kim.

I didn't know what to expect for a mall in South Africa. The Claremont Mall was for the people living here as opposed to the touristy V & A Mall.

"Don't take this wrong, Kim, but I didn't realize there were malls in Africa. Most of what we see on TV never shows this—only the poverty."

"What you see on TV is true for many parts of Africa, even South Africa. Even though our citizens have problems; in comparison, South Africa's economy is much more stable than other countries on the continent."

"We have the opposite problem. People from other countries somehow think all of the United States is like Beverly Hills with people living in mansions and wearing designer clothes. That's certainly not the case." Perhaps Dad was right, and the year in South Africa will teach me more than I could ever learn from a book.

The Claremont Mall had the usual stores, movie theatres, coffee shops, and eateries ranging from fast foods to the more expensive restaurants. The place was alive with the buzz of people.

"We're supposed to meet everyone in front of the restaurant in Financial Square," said Kim. We took the escalator to the upper level, found our meeting place, and stood by a large terra cotta pot that contained some type of palm tree. I wondered if Trudy would show up.

Kim must have read my mind. "Don't mind Trudy, Shelly. She considers Laura to be her best maat and gets jealous if Laura shows attention to anyone else."

"What's a maat?" I asked.

"Oh, that's what we call a friend. Anyway, Trudy doesn't understand that a person can have several friends."

"Does she consider me as some sort of threat?"

"Probably," Kim answered as she looked around to see if she could spot any of the other girls. "She's very insecure."

I waited a few seconds and then asked, "Does she get jealous over you girls?"

"Not really, she's used to having us around. We've all been friends for several years. She doesn't like to add anyone new to the group. Hey, that's her issue, not yours. I think I see Lacey now."

Coming from what looked like the food court, I saw Lacey heading our way. She sported the same big smile she had when I first met her in the cafeteria. I didn't have an opportunity to get to know her and hoped this afternoon would push that along.

"Hi, sorry I'm late. Laura, Hannah, and Trudy aren't here yet?" Well, that answered my unasked question. Trudy's coming. This should be a hoot. Lacey continued to smile as she touched my arm and gave it a slight squeeze. "Hi Shelly, glad you could make it."

"Thanks, Lacey. I'm really excited you asked me. It's not easy being so far away from home."

"Well, for now, think of Cape Town as your home," answered Lacey. "Here come the others."

I looked in the direction Lacey pointed and saw the three other girls rushing toward us. "We're so sorry we're late, but we got caught in a chocka block," announced Laura.

"No worries, just got here ourselves," said Lacey.

"Uh, what's a chocka block?" I asked.

"That's what we call a traffic jam," explained Kim. "I'm teaching Shelly how to speak English," Kim joked.

"Don't mind Kim. She likes to tease," said Laura.

I nodded my head as the five of us headed over to Woolies. We found our way to the handbag department and checked out the newest additions.

"Looks like you have Coach Bags here," I pointed out.

"You know, South Africa isn't totally backwards," Trudy threw back at me as she walked over to the jewelry counter.

"Oh no, I didn't mean that," I said. It seemed like I spent most of my time apologizing to this person. I walked over to the wallets and pretended to be interested in them. Hannah decided to try on a sweater in the dressing room while Kim and Laura continued looking at the handbags. I looked over at Trudy just in time to see her slip a bracelet in her pocket. I waited to see if she would put it back or pay for it. She did neither. Trudy turned around and caught me watching her. She knew I saw everything. What do I do now?

"Hey girls," Hannah called out putting the sweater back on the rack. "Is anyone ready for some lunch?"

We walked out of Woolies and over to a restaurant with tables set up in front to resemble an outdoor café. We sat down and looked at the menu. I caught Trudy staring at me as I ordered a burger. My no-response to Trudy's shoplifting definitely had me at the top of a coward's list. I needed to say something, but what and when? I certainly didn't want to be hanging out with someone who just shoplifted. I knew the other girls were unaware.

All day I troubled over what I witnessed. Shoplifting was a major problem for stores, and I had never been with someone who had actually done it. Being the new girl in town, I hesitated passing this information to Laura and Kim. Did I want to risk losing their friendship? Then again, did I want to be part of Trudy's group? I needed Amy's advice.

Chapter Twenty-Two
Trudy

"Over here, Shelly," Kim motioned as I entered the cafeteria carrying a tray of tomato soup and a toasted cheese sandwich. I carefully walked it over without spilling any of the soup onto my sandwich. I hated soggy toasted cheese.

"Hi, everyone." I managed to muster a smile as I sat next to Hannah. Trudy's presence at the table didn't go unnoticed. Neither did the glare coming from her squinty eyes. The lunch conversation went from the math test that took place that morning to the latest gossip about people I didn't know.

A half hour later I hurried down the hall to Spanish when a hand tapped me on the shoulder. I turned around and saw Trudy. "You say one word about the mall and you'll regret it."

I didn't like being threatened. So instead of cowering, I

decided to look her straight in the eye and said, "Say what about the mall? Oh, you mean how you stole a bracelet? By the way, are you wearing it?"

"You think you're pretty clever, don't you?"

"Not really, but if there's one thing I know I'm not, it's a thief."

Trudy pulled me over to the side of the long corridor and said, "Listen, new girl, no one would ever believe you. Why should they? We don't know anything about you. You might be a pathological liar for all we know."

No question about it—this girl was weird. Why didn't the other girls recognize this? Were they like her and I just hadn't figured it out yet?

I had a hard time concentrating in Spanish. Trudy frightened me. What was she capable of doing? Every time I glanced over at her, I found her staring at me. I needed to talk to someone about this situation but had no idea who I could trust. Most of all, I couldn't stand the stares. So I kept quiet which is what Trudy banked on.

Later that evening, I stayed in my room on the pretence of doing homework. Instead, I wrote an email to Amy telling her about Saturday. It was unbelievable how I traded a nasty Kylie for a scary Trudy.

Knock Knock

"Shelly, phone call," yelled Mei.

"Okay, I'm coming."

"It's some girl named Laura," Mei whispered.

"Thanks, Mei. Hi, Laura."

"Hi Shelly, I'm calling with the information on the play tryouts. Are you still interested in trying out for *Les Miserables*?"

"I am. By the way, will Trudy be auditioning, too?"

"No, she's not interested in drama club," Laura said. I felt relieved hearing that bit of news. "There will be a general meeting after school on Thursday for anyone signed up."

"Should I be prepared to do a reading?"

"No, it's just an informational meeting. You arrived at a good time," laughed Laura. "So how is everything else going?"

"What do you mean?" I asked a little startled.

"You know, are you figuring things out at school okay?"

"Oh, that. Yeah, things are falling into place. I have a little bit of a problem with Spanish. It seems the class is ahead of me with idioms and the vocabulary is off a bit, but because I don't have to deal with math and science, I can spend more time on it."

"Wish I could help you out with that but I'm taking French. Hey, isn't Trudy in your class? Maybe she could tutor you until you catch up?"

"No, that's okay. I'll figure it out."

"Do you want me to mention it to her?" Laura persisted.

"NO! I mean... no. I really don't want to bother her. Senora Perez said she'll help me with anything I don't understand." There was a long pause. I knew Laura wasn't buying my explanation but she let it drop.

"Well, okay. I'll see you in history tomorrow morning."

"Sure thing and thanks for the call." I hung up the phone, walked back to my room and glanced at my computer to see if I received an email from Amy. I wished I could text her but I didn't have that capability, and my parents refused to pay extra for the international service. Just then I heard a knock.

"Yeah?"

"Shelly, can I come in?" It was my mother.

"Sure," I said turning off my computer.

My mom strolled in carrying a large bowl of popcorn and placed it on my desk. "I thought you might like some."

"Thanks, I'll eat it later."

"Since when do you turn down popcorn?" Mom asked as she sat on the edge of the bed.

"I'm just not hungry." I tried to avoid looking at her. Mom could read me like a book, and I didn't feel like being read.

"I'm getting vibes that there's something wrong," Mom said. "You've seemed preoccupied since Saturday. What's happening? Is it school? Are things going well?"

"Yeah, it's okay." I felt a little uneasy, so I walked over to the window pretending to be interested in the yard.

"Just okay? Did something happen at school? Why don't you tell me what the problem is?" She sure is good…annoying…but good.

"All right, but you have to promise you won't say or do anything about what I tell you."

"I don't know if I can do that, Shelly. It depends on what it is you tell me. I guess you just have to trust me."

I turned from the window, picked my armadillo up from the floor, and held him close. "The girls I met at Lesterford are really very nice except for this one. Her name is Trudy and she hates my guts."

"Shelly, how can you say that? You've only been in school one week."

"Mom, she does. She's nothing but mean to me."

"Do you see her a lot?"

"Pretty much it's lunch and Spanish. At lunch, she sits with the same group of kids. That alone is enough to ruin my appetite. Then in Spanish, I swear all she does is glare at me."

"Could you be imagining this, Shelly?"

"Trust me, Mom, I am not imagining this. It is for real."

"But why would she hate you?" Mom asked. "Hate is a strong word."

I got up and sat next to her on the bed. "Well, for starters, she doesn't like the idea that her little group of friends has welcomed me into the circle. Then Saturday at the mall I saw her steal a bracelet from the jewelry counter. She knew I saw her take it."

Mom sat there for a few seconds thinking about what I told her. "Do any of the other girls know she did that?"

"No, I'm pretty sure I'm the only one who saw her. Today she warned that if I told anyone, she would fight the charge. Plus, people would believe her over me because no one knows me here. So what do I do?"

"This Trudy has a problem. It's more than the bracelet, Shelly, there must be something else bothering her," Mom said.

"I don't want to be around her. I like the other girls, just not her."

Mom looked at me and shook her head. "I certainly wouldn't go to the mall with her anymore. If she ever shoplifts again and you're with her, you could be incriminated."

"That's what I thought, too."

"Is there a counselor at school you could speak to about this situation?"

"Mom, I've only been here a few days!"

"Be cautious, Shelly. Just be very cautious. I think this girl needs help. Staying quiet about this will not help her."

"I know. I need to figure this all out. Mom, don't say anything to Mrs. Broodryk."

"Honey, I don't even know Mrs. Broodryk that well."
She squeezed my hand, stood up and walked to the door. "I
have confidence you can handle this situation. I'm here if
you need me. Keep me posted, okay?"

Chapter Twenty-Three
Touring Cape Town

Hi Amy,

Here's a riddle for you. How do you spell stress? Answer: T-R-U-D-Y (lol). I managed to get through two weeks here without causing too much damage. Laura, Hannah, Kim and Lacey are really nice. I know you'd like them a lot. I try to ignore the T girl (trouble, tough, touchy, temperamental Trudy). Anyway, I decided not to say anything about the bracelet incident. That'll probably haunt me forever.

How are the driving lessons coming? Lucky you! It'll be forever before I'm able to get my permit. In the meantime, you'll have to drive me around when I return. Today we're checking out the sights in Cape Town. I'm psyched about going up Table Mountain. Gotta go. Say hi to everyone. Miss ya.

I turned off my computer and made my way into the kitchen. Mei was slurping the milk from the bottom of her cereal bowl. How annoying is that!

"Mei, use your spoon," Mom advised as she wiped down the stove. "Shelly, did you have any breakfast? We're leaving in five minutes."

"Yeah, I had a bagel a half hour ago. Are we going up Table Mountain?" I asked.

"I thought we would do that," Dad said. "Charlie, the fellow from work, suggested we also check out Greenmarket Square and the area around it. As soon as you're ready, come on out. I'll be waiting in the car."

Soon we were heading towards Table Mountain. I saw open land with private homes at the base of the mesa. This eventually led to switchback roads that opened up to a large parking area. We got out and looked up at the sandstone sediments that towered above us.

"This sedimentary rock was deposited about 450 million years ago," Mom read out of her Cape Town tour book. "At one time an ocean covered this area. Then when the water receded, the mountain was carved out by the effects of wind, rain, ice, and extreme temperatures."

"Like the Grand Canyon," I added.

"Well, yeah, but the canyon is much bigger," Dad said. "Hey, does anyone want to walk up? There are marked trails if you're up for it."

"I'm choosing the cable car," Mom said. "What about you, girls? Do you want to walk?"

"I'll pass on the walking," I said.

"Me, too," yelled out Mei as she closed the car door.

After getting our tickets, we stood in line and finally

squeezed onto the cable car with the rest of the people. Being the last one on, I stood by the glass window next to the door. It was amazing seeing the earth fade away as we moved upward along the cable wire. Once we reached the top, we walked around stray boulders that were scattered on the ground as though they were thrown there.

"Look! Down there—it's the ocean," Mei pointed out as we stood behind the stone wall. "Doesn't this place look like a bowl?"

"You're right—like your cereal bowl," said Mom. "The rim of the bowl could be the mountains, the ocean would be at the very bottom, and somewhere in between is the city."

"You know, when we were down below I never noticed people walking around at the top," I said.

"That's probably because we're so far up. Hey, is that Lion's Head over there?" Mom asked.

Dad looked in the direction Mom pointed and saw what appeared to be a butte. "Yeah, Lion's Head actually separates Sea Point and Camps Bay from the center of the city."

"Everything looks close to each other up here," I said.

A short time later we were back in the car driving the switchbacks heading toward Greenmarket Square. Once on Buttengracht Road, I looked to the left and saw signs of the African bush. Homes were positioned on the upper level of the hill with apartments situated in the middle.

"All the buildings at the bottom of this hill were built only in the last few years," Dad pointed out.

"You mean none of this existed?" Mom asked.

"Charlie told me what we're seeing now used to be nothing but parking lots. These buildings were built on what was once ocean land. Under the buildings are pumps that keep water from coming into the buildings."

Before long we were traveling down Darling Street. "The buildings here look very British," Mom said.

"See that building over there?" asked Dad. "That's where the people saw Nelson Mandela for the first time in 28 years. He stood right on that black balcony."

"Who's he?" Mei inquired.

"We're studying about him in history class," I said. "Nelson Mandela was elected as the first black president of the new South Africa, Mei."

"Why is it called the *new* South Africa?"

"There was a time when South Africa was not democratic," I explained. "Because we've been studying about the apartheid, our history class is going to Robben Island for a field trip."

"Nothing like studying about the apartheid right here in South Africa," Dad said. "When do you go?"

"In two weeks, which reminds me—I have a permission slip for you to sign."

"I think I can park right here," Dad said angling the car between two other vehicles at the side of the road.

"Where are we, Daddy?" Mei asked."

"We're near Greenmarket Square. Let's get out and walk around. There's a lot of history on these streets. Do you see that building over there on Government Avenue? That's the Iziko Slave Lodge."

"Is that where the slaves were auctioned off?" I asked.

"Actually, I believe that was across the street. This building housed the slaves who worked in the Company's Garden," Dad explained. "Today the Slave Lodge is a museum bringing awareness of the struggle for human rights in South Africa."

We walked across the road until we came to the Company's

Garden where we saw another large statue of Cecil Rhodes, but this one had him sitting on a horse.

"I know something about that person," said Mei.

"You do, do you. Tell us," said Dad.

"That Cecil guy died from being sick."

"How do you know that?" I asked.

"Because all four legs of the horse are on the ground," Mei proudly stated knowing she was telling me something I didn't know. "Last year my teacher said that if a statue of a horse had all legs on the ground it meant the rider died but wasn't killed. And if the horse had one foot in the air, that meant the soldier was wounded in battle, but didn't die until later."

"What if the horse had two legs up?" I asked.

"That meant he was killed in the battle. You guys didn't know that?" Mei asked as she put her hands on her hips.

"I did," said Dad, "but I'm not sure if it's true or just a legend."

"No matter, Mei," I said looking at the horse statue, "that's an awesome story."

"Over there is the Iziko Planetarium," Mom said.

I looked but couldn't see it very well. Next to it stood a large, unfinished building that was under construction. Reddish, steel framework and a crane blocked my view beyond that point. From Government Avenue, we walked down Church Street and turned right onto Long Street.

"That building sure is fancy," Mei said motioning toward the white wrought-iron balconies that wrapped around each of three levels of a building.

"Yeah, these buildings are built to resemble the Victorian buildings in London. That has to be Greenmarket Square over there," said Mom. Across the road I saw an open-air market within a treed area. Alongside a cobbled square, there were several stalls with vendors showing their colorful wares. I looked amongst the crafts, candles, and African clothing only to spot the many versions of the carved Big Five I received for my birthday several weeks ago.

"What's that?" I asked Mom as she picked up this large oval object.

"It's an ostrich egg. Isn't it amazing how they pulled out the yolk and then painted scenes of Africa on the outside shell? I especially like this one with the map of the African continent. Steven, wouldn't these make great gifts for people back home?"

"How would you get them back?" Dad asked.

Mom picked one up and studied it carefully. "You're right. Maybe I'll buy just one for us. Did you know one ostrich egg can make enough scrambled eggs to feed ten people?"

"Ten people? Wow! That's a lot of eggs," I said.

"This here is the historical area in Cape Town," Dad said. "A long time ago ships passing the Cape stopped, traded their goods, and stocked up on produce before they continued on with their journey."

"You know, I've heard about the explorers traveling around Cape Town in their ships, but to be here seeing it as a real place…that's surreal."

Walking around, we found Greenmarket Square to be energized with people. No matter which stall we visited, we were greeted with a friendly smile and the invitation to barter. I quickly learned not to pay the price they first gave, but to instead bargain with them.

An hour later, we worked our way over to a pedestrian area called St. George's Mall. We stopped to watch the dancers, musicians, and other street entertainers. At the end of Adderley Street was Trafalgar Place named after the famous square in London. That's where we found the flower sellers. Colors of red, yellow, orange, and green flashed before us as the flowers were bunched in buckets of water.

Once we were back in the car, we voted to return home. We were tired but it was a good tired.

Chapter Twenty-Four
Trudy's Ire

"Los muchachos y las muchachas, en dos días ustedes tomarán una prueba española," Senora Perez announced. "Esté seguro de estudiar para esta prueba. Le veré mañana." *(Boys and girls, in two days you will take a Spanish test. Be sure to study for this test. I will see you tomorrow).*

I gathered my books and headed for the door.

"So Shelly, are you ready for the exam?"

I cringed hearing Trudy's voice. I decided I wouldn't be overly friendly to her, but I also didn't want to be rude. "I hope so," I said. "You guys are way ahead of where I was at my other school, so I've been trying to get caught up."

"I heard Senora Perez is helping you after school," Trudy said brushing past me at the door.

"Yeah, my parents arranged for her to tutor me until I caught up."

"I bet she gave you some hints for the test," Trudy said as though I knew something she didn't.

"No, not really. We've been going over the work that wasn't familiar. I'd come with questions and she'd explain. Plus she'd go over the homework with me. That's all."

"Yeah, whatever—see you around." And with that, Trudy took off down the hall in the opposite direction.

"That certainly was weird," I thought half out loud.

"Shelly, wait up." I looked over my shoulder only to see Laura working her way through the crowded hallway.

"Are you heading for drama club?" she asked.

"Yeah, I'm going to try out for the chorus ensemble. I don't think I can handle a large speaking part right now. I'm having all I can do to keep up in Spanish."

"No worries, Shelly. There really aren't that many parts for girls in this play anyways. I thought I would try out for either Cosette or Fantine."

"Well, good luck with it." We walked down the aisle to the seats in front of the stage.

"Let's all sit down," Mrs. Patterson announced tapping her pen on her clipboard. I couldn't help be amused. I noticed how similar drama coaches all appeared to be—a little eccentric and definitely dramatic.

"Before I hand out the scripts for your review, I want to make sure everyone understands the storyline behind *Les Miserables*. First of all, this is the musical version of Victor Hugo's classic. The storyline is the same, but some changes have been made in order to adapt it to a play. The setting is in Paris during the time of the French Revolution. Life then was scary. People were both angry and hungry, while the royals attended banquets and flaunted their riches in front of the poor. Are you familiar with the characters and where they fit into the whole picture?" asked Mrs. Patterson.

"No, I'm not," said this guy sitting in the front row. I looked over at him and thought he was awfully cute.

"Who's that?" I asked Laura.

"Oh, that's Spence Butler. Isn't he cute?" Laura giggled.

"Yeah, what's the story on him?"

"Spencer came here several years ago from England. His dad works for some bank. He used to go out with Mallory but then she moved back to Australia. You might say a lot of the girls at Lesterford wouldn't mind taking her spot, but he doesn't seem too interested. Why? You want to meet him?"

"Oh no, not really…I mean…just curious."

"I see," Laura said as she nudged my arm. "Stand in line!"

"Does anyone know who the main characters are?" asked Mrs. Patterson. "What about you, Robert? Any ideas?"

"I would say definitely Jean Valjean and Inspector Javert."

"That's right," said Mrs. Patterson. "Jean Valjean escapes from prison after stealing a loaf of bread to feed his sister's family. Inspector Javert is obsessed with finding this fugitive. Years later, Valjean becomes a prominent citizen, owns a successful factory, and is the mayor of the village."

"Isn't that when Javert discovers Valjean?" asked Robert.

"Well, he has his suspicions, but no definite proof."

"So what happens? Does he get caught?" asked Spence.

Laura nudged my arm and whispered, "Don't you love his British accent?"

"Yeah, this will make coming to play rehearsal more interesting. What a switch from Jeffrey!"

"Who's Jeffrey?"

"Some guy back home. Shh…I'll explain later. Mrs. Patterson's looking at us."

"Well," Mrs. Patterson said, "Valjean becomes friendly with Fantine, one of the factory workers. Soon she becomes very ill and fears she will die leaving her young daughter, Cosette, an orphan. Valjean promises to raise her as his own."

"Who's Marius?" asked this guy named Martin.

"Marius is a militant student. Years later, Marius and Cosette fall in love and get married," explained Mrs. Patterson.

"I'm trying out for that part," Martin said with a grin on his face.

Mrs. Patterson ignored Martin's remark as she sat down on her high stool in front of the stage. "Now I want to tell you about another character who is rather colorful. Her name is Themardier. Whoever gets that part has to act a little quirky. She accuses Valjean as being a murderer, and claims that on the night the barricades fell, she saw him steal a ring from a corpse in the sewers. It's not especially a long part but it can be quite fun."

"Shelly, you should try out for that part—Thermardier. It sounds like it might be just what you're looking for," Laura whispered in my ear.

"Are you insinuating that I'm quirky?" At that we both started to laugh until we noticed Mrs. Patterson looking in our direction. Amazing how a teacher's evil eye can produce silence.

Mrs. Patterson handed me my script and asked, "Are you new?"

"I've been here a month," I answered.

"You sound American. What brings you to South Africa?"

"Yeah, I am. We're here for a year. My dad's doing environmental research at the university."

"I see. What's your name?"

"Shelly—Shelly Kilpatrick."

"Well, Miss Shelly Kilpatrick, just a couple of suggestions. First of all, we say yes and not yeah. And from now on, you don't laugh and talk when you should be listening."

I could have died right on the spot. What a terrible impression I'm making at this new school. All I could muster was a simple, "I'm sorry, Mrs. Patterson. It won't happen again."

I made my way through the crowded hallway feeling rather crummy. As I walked past the Spanish room, I noticed Trudy leaving with a blue folder tucked in her arms. She carefully shut the door, looked both ways, and quickly sped to her locker. She appeared nervous and I wondered why she had such a strange look on her face.

The next day came soon enough. Nothing seemed out of the ordinary until lunch. I placed my books on my stool; then walked over to the other side of the room to throw away my garbage. When I returned it appeared Trudy had accidentally knocked everything of mine onto the floor.

"I am so sorry, Shelly. I guess I'm getting a little clumsy." She picked everything up and placed them neatly back onto the stool.

"No problem," I said as I picked up the books and headed to Spanish. When I walked into the room I noticed Senora Perez looked upset. Normally she stood by the door and greeted each of us as we arrived. Today she sat quietly at her desk.

"Class, before we begin today's lesson, I need to talk to you. It appears that sometime between yesterday's class and this morning, someone made off with the answer key to tomorrow's Spanish test. I do not enjoy accusing anyone, but I believe it might have been someone from this room. I know I didn't misplace it, and I never took the answer key out of the room. So if someone doesn't come forward, there will be serious consequences for the entire class."

All of us sat quietly and looked at each other. Who could have done that? Just then Trudy raised her hand. "Senora Perez, what does the answer key look like?" she asked.

"It's in a blue folder, Trudy."

"Blue folder?" I thought. Trudy came out of the Spanish room with a blue folder yesterday afternoon. I remember thinking how weird she acted.

"Well, Senora, is this it?" Trudy asked as she pointed to a blue folder squeezed into a pile of books that lay on the floor under my chair. She pulled out the folder and handed it to Senora Perez.

"Shelly, I need to speak to you after class," Senora Perez said with a surprised look on her face.

"Senora, I don't know how that got into my things. Seriously, I didn't take it."

"We'll talk about this later," she said as she placed the answer key in her top drawer and started the lesson.

After class, everyone filed out of the room, and I walked over to Senora Perez's desk. "Senora, I didn't take the answer key but I believe I know who did." I went on to explain everything that happened between Trudy and me from the time I first met her—the cold reception I've received from her; the theft of the bracelet at the mall; and my observation of Trudy leaving the empty Spanish room after drama club. I also relayed how a few minutes before Spanish she tipped my books onto the floor in the cafeteria as I went to throw out my garbage.

Senora Perez listened with interest. She said she needed to call Trudy down to the headmaster's office and all of us would discuss this situation together. "You better call your mother, Shelly, to let her know you'll be arriving home later than usual. Better yet, ask her to join us." I could not believe what was unfolding. Mom was right. I should have spoken up about Trudy as soon as I saw her take the bracelet. Now I'm in the middle of a big mess.

Sitting outside Mr. Barratt's office, Trudy's words, "You say one word about the mall and you'll regret it," played continuously inside my head. Well, I didn't say anything about what I saw at the mall; yet I'm still regretting it. I looked up from counting the linoleum tiles on the floor only to see Trudy staring at me with her cold eyes.

Just then the door opened and in walked my mom. "Shelly, what's this all about?"

Seeing my mom, ripped apart my defenses. I couldn't stop; the tears flowed.

"Mom, I was never in any trouble back at Jackson High School. I'm here for a month and I have that girl over there out to get me, the drama coach telling me to respect her when she talks, and my Spanish teacher thinking I stole the answer key to the test we're taking tomorrow."

"Whoa, wait a minute. Let's start this conversation over. I think I'm missing a few pieces of the puzzle."

"Mrs. Kilpatrick, Trudy, Shelly—would you step into my office, please?" asked Mr. Barratt. Inside sat Senora Perez.

"Please everyone, take a seat. Mrs. Kilpatrick, there's a situation we need to resolve. Senora Perez informed me that the answer key to an exam she planned on giving tomorrow came up missing, and she found it in Shelly's pile of books."

"Mr. Barratt, can I say something?" I interrupted.

"Go ahead, Shelly."

"Don't you think it's a little strange that right after Senora explained how her folder was taken, Trudy immediately noticed it in a pile of books under my seat? Do you really think I would carry the answer key to class if I truly took it? Wouldn't that be stupid of me? Also, don't you think it's coincidental that Trudy knocked over my books in the cafeteria; then tried to straighten them out...right before Spanish class?"

"She's framing me," yelled Trudy. "She's the one who took the answer sheet and now she's blaming me. She told me herself she felt unprepared for the test because she was behind in the work."

"Trudy, let Shelly speak and then you'll have your turn," Mr. Barratt said. "Go ahead, Shelly." I looked over at Trudy and could see daggers coming from her piercing eyes. Somehow, I no longer felt afraid of her and I think she knew it.

"Yesterday, as I walked to my locker, I noticed Trudy coming out of the Spanish room carrying a blue folder. It was near the end of the day because I was leaving the auditorium. She didn't see me, but I saw her. I didn't think much about it at the time, but I did wonder why she was in such a big hurry."

"Trudy, now it's your turn. What do you have to say about all of this?"

"Sir, Shelly has been nothing but trouble since she came here. She keeps accusing me of doing stuff I never did."

"Like stealing from the mall?" asked Senora. Stunned, Trudy immediately stopped talking.

"You told them I stole a bracelet?" Trudy yelled.

"Trudy, I never mentioned a bracelet—you did," said Senora Perez.

"Shelly and Mrs. Kilpatrick, could you step outside please?" asked Mr. Barratt.

We got up and quietly walked out of the office. I went over to a corner of the waiting room to try and get out of the range of curious stares. The phones rang amongst the announcements over the PA system. Normally none of that would be a problem, but today it flustered me. I used this time to explain to Mom what transpired since our last Trudy conversation.

"Shelly, if you didn't take the folder, you have nothing to worry about."

"Mom, IF I didn't take the folder?"

"I'm sorry, I know you didn't. You've never given us any reason to doubt you before. So, in this situation, I have to believe that what you're saying is true."

After what seemed like an eternity, the door to Mr. Barratt's office opened and Senora Perez walked out. "Shelly, Trudy has admitted to everything."

"But why did she do that to me?" I asked.

"She wanted to get you into trouble. You are exonerated of any guilt and are free to go home. Lesterford takes stealing and cheating seriously. I'm asking you, however, not to say anything to any of your friends about this matter. The situation will be resolved, but we don't want it to be fodder for gossip."

"I won't, Senora, I promise." My mom and I got up to walk out. "Senora?"

"Yes, Shelly?"

"I hope Trudy won't be expelled. She has problems, and now would be a good time for her to deal with them."

"Mrs. Kilpatrick, you have a remarkable young lady here," said Senora Perez.

"Thanks, Senora. We know that but it's nice to hear it

from other people."

Once in the car I said, "You know, Mom, I know how Jean Valjean felt after being accused of stealing that ring in the sewer. It was horrible being blamed for something I never did. I felt so helpless."

"Shelly, if it wasn't for the migraine I'm experiencing right now, I would ask you who this Jean person is and exactly what it is you're talking about."

"He's the main character in *Les Miserables*. You know, the play the junior class is putting on." At that moment, the two of us broke into some well-needed laughter.

"Oh Shelly, for a brief moment you had me worried. Let's go home."

Chapter Twenty-Five
Robben Island

"All right students, board the bus," Mrs. Van Wyk said as we walked from the school to the parking lot out back. I pulled my jacket closer to me and climbed the steps of the bus. A small calendar attached to the panel next to the driver showed September, but here in South Africa it was late winter. My mind wandered to the early autumn weather Amy and Natalie must be enjoying in the states.

Laura sat next to me as we took our places on the bus. We were studying about the apartheid and Robben Island was a part of that historical period that took place a few decades ago. Names such as Nelson Mandela, Hector Pieterson, and Freedom Square filled the pages of the books we read in class. I knew of the apartheid—even last spring had a few lessons on it at Jackson High, but I didn't have a total understanding of it all. Most likely the kids in South Africa never spent months learning about the pilgrims and the Boston Tea Party either as we did in America.

"Shelly, what happened with Trudy? I heard there was a huge problem between the two of you in Spanish—something about a stolen answer sheet."

"I can't talk about it, Laura. I promised I wouldn't. I can tell you Senora cleared my name, and if you want to hear anything more you'll have to ask Trudy."

"I called her but she won't come to the phone," said Laura. "She's been out of school for several days now. Her brother said she's sick." Laura looked at me as she said all this, but I didn't respond. The last thing I needed was for Senora Perez to discover I broke my promise and blabbed. That was not going to happen.

"Well, I can see you're not talking," Laura said.

I nodded my head and to change the subject asked, "Where do we pick up the boat to Robben Island?"

"Not far. We have to go down by the V & A Waterfront."

Mrs. Van Wyk sat up front with a microphone. "Okay, kids, a few things about what you'll see this morning. Robben Island started out being a prison settlement. It was named Robbe Eiland by the Dutch in the mid 17th century. Does anyone know how it got that name? Ben?"

"Somebody named Robert named it?" answered Ben. The kids on the bus chuckled as Ben enjoyed the attention. However, Mrs. Van Wyk didn't appear too amused.

"No, Ben. Would anyone else care to answer? Margot?"

"I read an article about it in a magazine. It said the name meant seal island because at one time there were so many seals over there."

"That's correct, Margot. Later the island became a leper colony. During World War II it changed into an artillery garrison. And in 1960 it returned to being a prison but for people who opposed apartheid. One of its most famous prisoners was, of course, Nelson Mandela. Today it actually serves as a museum and nature reserve."

"When did it stop being a prison, Mrs. Van Wyk?" asked Laura.

"1991—which was before you were born, but I remember it like it was yesterday."

"What exactly will we be seeing over there?" I asked.

"For one, there's the prison itself. But the island also serves as a breeding colony for more than 130 bird species."

"My dad said there are a lot of rabbits over there," yelled out Ben.

"He's right about that. They're actually a huge nuisance and occasionally the island will close so that some of them can be trapped. Oh, looks like we've arrived at the ferry. Stay together and follow me. I have your tickets."

The boat ride over was fun even though the wind was sharp. Most of us sat inside with only a few daring people on the outside top deck. A TV, mounted on the wall, showed a documentary film about the prison. A few kids listened but mostly everyone talked amongst themselves.

As the boat docked, a bus pulled over to pick us up. A fairly large man climbed aboard and introduced himself as an ex-political prisoner. It turned out that he was our guide who would take us around the island.

"If you look to your right, you'll see the Governor's House. Today it's used as a conference center." What I spotted was a Victorian styled, stone building with a large porch. At the top of its red and white roof, was a fairly large cupola with many windows. In front were two large anchors positioned one on each side of the walkway leading up to the front porch.

A little further down the road we arrived at the lighthouse. "This lighthouse was built in the late 1800's," our guide said. "Its beam can be seen from a distance of 25 km." I quietly used my math to do a quick conversion and figured that to be about 15 miles.

When the guide talked, I had to listen closely as he spoke a language that was part English and part Afrikkan. "On the left we'll be passing the Church of the Good Shepherd which was put up by the lepers that lived here in the late 1800's. Since there were no pews or chairs back then, they had to stand when they came to worship."

I saw a sandy brown church built of stone—plain but beautiful. I tried to imagine what it must have been like for those people who were outcasts of society. It had to be hard for them, not just physically but also emotionally.

"Soon we'll be passing the lime quarry where most of us prisoners worked, even Nelson Mandela. It was hard labor but if we didn't produce, we faced physical beatings," the guide said. The view of the quarry from the window looked pretty desolate to me. No trace of color or life seemed to exist in this mined area. Everything was white.

"Laura, I wonder if the lime ever got into their lungs or the pores of their skin?"

"Or their eyes," Laura added. "I don't understand how anyone could tolerate this place, year after year."

"Laura, look at that cool bird!"

"Which one?"

"Over there; its head is black on top and white on the bottom with a red beak."

"That's a Caspian Tern," Laura said. "There are a lot of them over here."

Shortly after, our bus pulled up to the prison itself. We got off and followed our guide through a door into what looked like an enclosed prison yard. The top third of the prison walls were white stucco while the lowered section consisted of dark stone pieces mortared together.

"Here is where the prisoners were taken for fresh air and exercise," the guide said. "Political and common law prisoners lodged together at first. But in 1971, the political prisoners became further isolated. The officials limited our only contact with the outside world to sending and receiving two letters a year."

"Only two letters?" inquired Margot. "That's all?"

"That's all." Everyone quietly stood as each person tried to digest the information we received. "In addition to the beatings, hard physical labor in the quarry, and solitary confinement, we also suffered from insufficient food, bedding and few changes of clothing," the guide continued. "Let's go inside and I'll show you Nelson Mandela's cell located in Section B."

We eagerly followed him only to stop at the end of a long, narrow hallway. On both sides I could see the continuous pattern of a wooden door and window. The little bit of light coming from the ceiling reflected onto the tiled floor. Only one of those doors remained open—the door to Nelson Mandela's cell. I peeked inside and saw a closet-sized room with a cot, sink and one sole table holding a tin plate and cup. I imagined Nelson Mandela looking out of the small, barred window onto the courtyard day after day, year after year.

"This is so sad," I whispered to Laura. Laura nodded her head.

"Robben Island," the guide continued, "was used to isolate opponents of apartheid and to crush their spirit. Nelson Mandela spent 27 years of his life in prison for his beliefs. He once wrote, 'It was once a place of darkness, but out of that darkness has come a wonderful brightness, a light so powerful that it could not be hidden behind prison walls.'"

"You know, Laura," I whispered, "that's true for so many people who have sacrificed their lives for causes they believed in. I never thought about it before, but your country has martyrs and heroes, too."

Laura smiled and said, "Yeah, we all have our Ben Franklins and Abraham Lincolns. Many people in South Africa hold Nelson Mandela with much respect. But in addition to him, there are many less familiar people who have sacrificed much to make things better."

The ride back to Cape Town on the large, white catamaran was unusually quiet.

Everyone was battling their own personal thoughts and feelings. Once we were on the bus Mrs. Van Wyk asked for our impressions. Most everyone wanted to talk about the experience.

"Mrs. Van Wyk," I said, "the conditions the prisoners had to endure were physically hard, but how did they keep themselves together emotionally? It must have been extremely difficult."

"Good observation, Shelly. If your family is ever in Johannesburg you might want to take a ride over to Soweto where the apartheid massacre took place."

"Is that a town?" I asked.

"Yes, Soweto is about ten miles southwest of Johannesburg. The name itself comes from an acronym. The SO in Soweto stands for South. The WE stands for West and the

TO in Soweto comes from Township. Put the pieces together and you have Southwest Township or the name Soweto."

That evening at dinner, I found it difficult not to talk about what I experienced. "Did you know that during the apartheid there were four classes of people?"

"Four?" asked Mom.

"Uh huh—the Blacks, Coloureds, Indians, and Whites."

"Who made up the Indians and the Coloureds?" Mom asked.

"The Indians were mostly the Asian people," I answered.

"That would be me," Mei said.

"Yeah, I guess that would be you, Mei. And the Coloureds were people of mixed race. These four groups were treated differently. Mrs. Van Wyk said there were different laws for each race group—like the black people were not allowed to vote or express themselves."

"From what I heard," Dad added, "if they were working in what was designated as a "white" area they had to have some type of identification or they would be arrested."

"That's what Mrs. Van Wyk said, too. It was called a passbook. They weren't allowed to move about freely and could only stay in their area. She also said that very few people had electricity or water."

"Wasn't it invented yet?" Mei asked.

"No, it was. It's just the blacks didn't have it," I explained. "During apartheid, the Coloureds were considered higher than the Blacks, but lower than the Whites."

"So, Shelly, what happened in Soweto?" asked Dad. "You're getting it right from the source while most of us only learned from newspaper accounts."

"We were quite young when the apartheid took place. I

never really grasped the complexity of the problems," added Mom.

"Mrs. Van Wyk said the black students in Soweto were protesting against the use of the Afrikaans language in their schools. There was a law that forced all black schools to use Afrikaans when teaching math and social studies. English would be used for science and things like needlework and woodwork. The Sowetan kids didn't want to be taught in Afrikaans—they wanted English. So one morning thousands of black students walked from their schools to Orlando Stadium to protest at a peaceful rally."

"When was that, Shelly?" asked Mom.

"In 1976—June 16."

"Shelly, June 16th is your birthday," Dad said.

"Yeah, that's how I remembered the date."

"Speaking of birthdays, does anyone want ice cream for dessert?" Mom asked.

"Me!" yelled Mei.

Mom got up and walked to the freezer. "So Shelly, why did this peaceful rally end in a massacre?"

"What's a massacre?" Mei asked.

"Well, how should I put this?" Mom said. "It's when lots of people get killed."

"Were kids killed, too?" Mei asked.

I looked over at Mei and nodded my head. "Once they started marching, they found the road they were on was barricaded by the police so they continued in a different direction. All the while they sang and held signs with slogans written on them."

"How did they die?" Mei persisted.

"Things got ugly when some of the kids started throwing stones. The police used dogs and tear gas to disperse the students, but that didn't work. Soon they found themselves surrounded by the crowd, panicked and a couple of shots were fired into the crowd."

"Is that when people were killed?" Mei asked.

I looked at Mei and realized how truly bothered she was hearing all this. "Mei, this happened many years ago, but it's part of South Africa's history."

"That's right, Mei," said Dad. "Many countries have stories from their past that they're not particularly proud of."

"I know, Daddy. Keep going, Shelly. Tell us more." Mom looked over at me and nodded her approval to continue.

"When the police fired shots, the students screamed and that resulted in more shots. Soon rioting started and about twenty-three people died, but the number wounded was over a thousand."

"How many kids got killed?" asked Mei.

"Several," I answered. "One in particular was Hector Pieterson. Actually, there's a famous picture of this man carrying him down the street right after he was shot."

"How old was he, Shelly?" Mei asked.

"Hector was twelve years old."

"That's smaller than you, Shelly."

"Yeah, way smaller. Anyway, this uprising was considered the turning point in the apartheid struggle. Fourteen years later, the people elected the ANC party into office and made Nelson Mandela their new president."

"The guy in jail?" Mei asked.

"Yeah."

"Is this a true story?"

"What do you mean, Mei?"

"Like sometimes stories are interesting but they aren't really true."

"Are you wondering if it really happened?" I asked.

"Yeah."

"It did."

"And you know," Dad added, "all of that happened not very long ago. So often the events and people we read about took place hundreds or even thousands of years back. But with this conflict, you can go to Soweto and actually meet up with adults who were students in that very same march."

"Getting the facts from an eyewitness makes this story especially moving," Mom added.

"I know. Hearing both Mrs. Van Wyk and the Robben Island ex-prisoner tell us about the apartheid was much better than just reading it out of a history book. You know, lots of kids hate history. At least I did. But, I don't know, I guess I no longer think about history as being so boring anymore. It never dawned on me that all that stuff really happened. Like I knew it did, but it never sunk in."

"What are your thoughts about it now?" Dad asked.

"Right now I think history's amazing."

"It's not always easy shifting from the present to the past," Dad said. "But it's been proven that one of the best ways to prevent current problems is to check out the mistakes made by people before us."

"History repeats itself," Mom said.

"I guess the patterns are there if we look for them," Dad added.

With that, I nodded my head and placed my spoon into a bowl of melted ice cream.

Chapter Twenty-Six
A Quick Solution

"**O**kay, Shelly, I think we have it all set to go." Dad downloaded the program that will allow me to not only talk to my friends back home but also see them.

"I'm so excited about this," I said as I jumped into the seat in front of the computer. "Erin invited Amy and Natalie over so we could chat with each other."

"Okay, it's sending the signal and hopefully your friends will be on the other end," Dad said.

"Shelly!" Erin yelled. "I can see you! This is so amazing."

"Hi Shelly, we're here, too. Can you see us?" yelled Natalie and Amy.

"I can, you guys look great! I miss you so much."

"Okay, looks like you're good here," said Dad. "Hi girls, I'm leaving and will let you catch up."

"Hi Mr. Kilpatrick," Amy yelled over the cyberlines halfway around the world.

"Amy, you have a new haircut," I said looking into the monitor as though she were inside. "I love it!"

"Thanks...hey, what's new, girlfriend?"

"Oh, managing okay. Actually, it's pretty awesome here. Are you back in school?"

"We are," said Erin. "Sounds like you never stopped."

"Yeah, I just finished my third term. We had exams and now I have a week off before the fourth term. Can you believe that?"

"That is so weird," said Amy.

"Have you seen my buddy, Kylie Brezman?" I laughed. "Does she miss me?"

"Oh yeah," said Natalie. "She has no one to jerk around now that you're gone."

"I'm sure she doesn't miss the competition," said Erin. "I'll let you know if she tries out for this year's play."

"Oh, the play. Do you know what they're putting on?" I asked.

"I think it's *Romeo and Juliet*. You can be sure she'll be going for the Juliet part," said Natalie with a beefed up, sarcastic voice.

"If she gets it, I hope Jeff Rickerson is Romeo," said Amy.

"You girls are sooo bad. That's why I miss you."

"Hey, how's it going in South Africa? Are you still having a problem with that Trudy girl?" Amy asked.

"Isn't she the one who tried to sabotage you?" asked Erin.

"There seems to be one in every school, no matter where you live," said Natalie.

"Yeah, she no longer goes to Lesterford," I said looking down at the floor.

"What happened?" asked Amy.

"Well, it's a long story but after the answer sheet situation, I told my Spanish teacher that I didn't want anything bad to happen to her. But the rumor I'm hearing is that Mr. Barratt, the headmaster, expelled her."

"No way!" said Erin.

"Yeah, I feel really bad about all that, but honestly? Life's a lot easier for me with her gone. Do you think that's terrible for me to say?"

"Shelly, I'd say more than that if I had been in your shoes," Natalie said.

"Well, no matter, I hope she's getting help. She has major issues. Oh, not to change the subject but my dad is going to Kruger National Park for his job. He'll be there for four days. Because we have the week off from school, we're going with him."

"Oh, that is so cool," said Natalie.

"Where is Kruger?" asked Erin.

"Kruger is near Johannesburg which is pretty far from Cape Town. We're going to fly there. Amy, remember how you asked me if I would be going on a safari while over here? We'll be doing one at Kruger."

"How I would love to do that," said Amy.

"My mom signed us up. I'll let you know what it's like. Oh, I have a question for you. Are Josh Zettleman and Caroline Fenster still going out?"

"Actually, they broke up again," Erin answered. "Are you interested?"

"No way and don't tell anyone I asked. I was just curious."

"Are there any cute guys there?" asked Amy.

"Yeah, there are," I said, "but haven't seen anyone that's special yet."

"Hey Shelly, guess what? I got my driver's license," Natalie said giving the thumbs up.

"That's awesome, Natalie. Have you driven around on your own yet?"

"We're going to the mall tomorrow," Erin announced.

"It took some convincing to get my parents to let me drive the girls. Pretty much had to agree to everything that there's to agree on."

"Well, that's not happening here. I'll have to wait until I return to the states before I can even get my permit."

"Shelly, we have to sign off now," said Natalie. "Let's do this again. Maybe you can have Laura and the other girls there, so we can meet each other."

"Sounds like a plan. Bye! Miss you a lot!" I said feeling a little homesick.

"Bye, Shelly!" yelled the girls at the other end. I waved until their faces faded from the monitor. I sat there staring at an empty screen until I heard my door open.

"Shelly, what are you doing?" It was Mei. She always wants to know what I'm doing.

"I just finished talking to Natalie, Erin and Amy." I stood up and started to leave my room when I noticed Mei wasn't her usual bouncy self. "Is something wrong?"

"I don't know. I kinda miss Jennifer."

"Oh...I see. You know, I miss my friends, too."

"It's different for you."

"How's that?"

"You have lots of friends here—Laura, Hannah, Lacey and Kim."

"Mei, you have friends. I always hear you talk about Lindsey and Samantha."

"They're my school friends. I don't have anyone near my house to play with like I did back home."

"Oh, a neighborhood friend; you miss that, huh?"

"Yeah."

"Did you tell Mom? Maybe she'll let you invite one of your school friends over to our house for a play date?"

"That's for little kids," Mei said.

"Oh, and now that you're six, play dates aren't cool. So how about sleepovers? They're still cool for me?"

"Maybe," said Mei as she climbed on my bed.

"How about playing a game of checkers? You want to be red or black?" With me being wrapped up in my own little crisis, it never occurred to me that Mei might not be adjusting to this move. As we set up the game, I decided I would mention this conversation to my parents.

We weren't very long into the game when I heard the phone ring. I started to jump up to get it, but then decided that might not be a good idea with Mei feeling so alone.

"Hey Mom, if it's for me, I'll call back later," I yelled from my bedroom. "It's your move, Mei."

A short time later Mom appeared at the door. "The call is for Mei."

"Mei?" I quickly caught myself from asking who would be calling her.

"For me?" Mei jumped up from the floor and raced out of the room. Once she left I described to Mom about what transpired only a short time ago. She agreed Mei should have a friend over from school and was all set to suggest it, when Mei came bursting back into the room with the announcement that she was invited to a birthday party. "Can I go?"

"Whose birthday is it?" Mom asked.

"Samantha's and guess what? She's inviting Lindsey and

two other girls from school. Can I go, please? She said her mom wants to talk to you."

Mom smiled and said, "Well, let's see what this is all about?"

In a matter of only a couple of minutes, I found myself alone in my room with an abandoned checker game on the floor. Everyone has problems. I guess no matter what size, they're big to the person experiencing them. I looked over at my stuffed armadillo and said, "How come Mei's problems are so quickly resolved, Miguel?"

"Who are you talking to, Shelly?" Mei asked coming back into my room.

"No one…just was mumbling to myself."

"Ya know, Shelly, if you're lonely—just ask someone to come for a sleepover."

Chapter Twenty-Seven
Hazyview

I wouldn't call the hotel in Hazyview an ordinary place. Resting only minutes outside one of Africa's largest animal preserves had something to do with it. The massive wall and fence surrounding its grounds offered a protective facade. On the other hand, my curiosity sparked as I imagined what could exist on the other side. From my perspective, we saw rows of nicely furnished rooms that opened onto freshly cut lawns and transplanted palm trees to give the impression of lush tropics. But in reality, this was the bush country—the savannah where lions, leopards, elephants, warthogs, buffalos and rhinos enjoyed hanging out.

After we settled into our room, Mei and I decided to take a walk around the hotel's grounds. We followed the brick walkway until we reached an outdoor pool surrounded by a grassy patio. This pool overlooked a lush valley with trees sporting purple blossoms. We walked over toward the pool and sat down on two of the mustard-colored, wicker chaise lounges. Matching umbrellas stuck into the ground next to small tables. I noticed the tan tile shaped from stone around the swimming pool where fallen purple blossoms floated in the water.

"What's that over there?" Mei asked. She pointed to a tree with weird straw balls hanging from it.

"I have no idea. They look like Japanese lanterns, don't they?"

A man pushing a luggage cart stopped when he overheard our conversation. "Good afternoon, misses. Those things you are wondering about are nests made by weavers."

"Are weavers—birds?" I asked.

"Yes, miss. The weavers make their nests so they hang down instead of being cradled in branches."

"That's cool."

"What kind of flowers are those?" Mei asked. Each had a long stalk bent at the neck with colorful, spear-like flowers fanning out at the end. "Don't they look like birds?"

"Good observation, little lady. That's the bird of paradise," the man answered.

"My friend at home has a plant like that but it grows indoors," I said.

"It's a warm climate plant," the man answered. "They grow very good outdoors in South Africa."

"What's that smell?" Mei asked wrinkling her nose.

"Oh yeah, you smell that, huh? That's creosote," the man explained as he smiled at Mei's reaction. "We put the creosote on the wooden fences to keep the termites from eating them. Termites like to eat wood. All over the savannah you will see large trees with mounds of dirt around their base. That's what's left over from the tree once the termites start feasting. Have you seen that yet?" Mei shook her head no. "Well, you keep your eyes open and you will."

"Can you tell us what the purple flowers are? They're everywhere," I asked.

"Those blossoms are part of a common tree here in South Africa. It's called the jackurenda. We have quite a few unique trees. Have you seen the mopane?"

"I don't know. What's that like?" I asked.

"They grow in the savanna. They're fairly tall and their limbs fan out. Look for them along the road and you might see baboons hiding in their branches."

"Baboons are loose here?" Mei asked.

The man laughed and said, "We have baboons and monkeys like you have chipmunks and squirrels! Well, misses, need to get me back to work. See you now. Have a lekker day."

"What did he say?" Mei asked after the man left.

"He said to have a lekker day. Lekker means nice. I learned that at school."

"There you girls are," Mom said as she and my dad approached us. "Isn't this a fantastic place?"

"Mom, those trees are jacku something and they have baboons in them."

"No, they're called jackurendas and the baboons are in the mopane trees," I said. "Dad, this man who works here told us about them and the weaver birds that build the nests you see over there."

"Hmm, interesting," said Dad. "Well girls, we're all set for our safari tomorrow morning. We'll have to hit the sack early because we're leaving at 5:30 sharp."

"Why so early?" I moaned.

"When you're on a safari you have to be on the animals' schedule. That's the time things start waking up in the bush.

They nap in the afternoon. Let's head off to dinner." We walked up the steps and into a large room divided by a dining station.

"Everything is beautifully displayed in these colorful dishes," Mom said picking up an olive-green salad bowl with oval shaped leaves painted on the side. Along the top edge were small, raised dots that formed triangular patterns. "Isn't this nice?"

"Sure," I said. The dishes didn't intrigue me as much as the food. "Do you know what this is?" I asked while pointing to a pot containing meat that looked like stew.

"Take a small spoonful to see if you like it." That's what Mom always says whenever we stare at something unrecognizable.

"That's potjie pot," the server said. "Potjie is a method of cooking stew in a barbeque pot." I put a small amount on my plate as Mom suggested.

"Okay everyone, what was your favorite part of the day?" Dad asked after we settled down to eat. This was a question that everyone had to answer at dinner.

"Hmm, this potjie pot stuff is good. Oh, favorite place? Easy, it was at the Canyon— the one with all those holes on the side walls."

"Oh, you mean the potholes of Bourke's Luck on the Blyde River Canyon," Dad said.

"Yeah...whatever...anyway, it was awesome—especially the paths leading over the bridges."

"Why was that your favorite?" asked Mom.

"I don't know. The rocks looked unreal...like nothing I've ever seen before."

"What's amazing about those potholes," Dad said, "is how long it took for the water and pebbles to wear away the rock."

"Water is a powerful force," Mom added. "So Mei, your turn, what was your favorite thing today?"

"I liked where we stopped for lunch."

"Pilgrim's Rest," Mom said.

"Yeah, exactly what was that town about?" I asked.

"Pilgrim's Rest showed what life was like a long time ago," said Dad.

"Oh, like Williamsburg and Cooperstown back home?" I asked.

"Yeah, all those restaurants and shops used to be old Victorian homes."

Mom pulled a wrinkled brochure out of her purse. "I picked this up in one of the little shops. It says, 'Pilgrim's Rest owes its existence to the first gold rush in South Africa.'"

"When was that?" I asked.

"It says '1873. By the end of that year more than 1500 gold diggers arrived and expanded the mining camp into a town.' I have to say Pilgrim's Rest is on my list of favorite places, too," said Mom. "Hard to believe those quaint Victorian cottages people built out of tin and timbers have lasted all these years. The town is certainly well preserved."

"The miners thought that once the gold was mined they would move on. But the gold lasted almost 100 years and so did Pilgrim's Rest," explained Dad.

"Pilgrim's Rest may have been surrounded by gold, but a miner's life was pretty simple," said Mom.

"I thought the Old Print House was a neat place," Dad added. "I guess the printers were one of the first residents that settled in the town."

"Why's that?" I asked.

"Because newspapers were the only way the residents received any news."

"That's not why I liked it there," said Mei.

Dad smiled and said, "All right, tell us, Mei. Why did you like Pilgrim's Rest?"

We all stopped talking and waited for Mei's answer. She appeared to enjoy the instant attention. "I liked the place we ate at. What was it called? They had the best toasted cheese and tomato sandwiches."

"The Fables Restaurant," said Dad.

"Yeah, that's it. I liked sitting outside at that picnic table with those pink umbrellas."

"Mei, you're good at remembering details," Mom joked.

"I just remember this lady standing on the sidewalk with a basket on her head."

"Oh yeah, she carried packages of macadamia nuts," I said.

"Yeah, maca…macamane…what's it called again?"

"Macadamia nuts," I repeated and we all laughed.

"Shelly, I have a question about her. Why was she smiling and pointing at me?"

"She wanted to sell you some."

"Oh, I didn't know that. What was your favorite thing, Daddy?"

"I have to side with Shelly. Being a science teacher, I liked the Blyde River Canyon. I only wish we had the time to walk the overnight trails."

"Where would we sleep?" I asked.

"There are places in Swadini," Dad said looking at his watch. "Talking about sleep, we better head back to the room. Five-thirty will come pretty darn fast."

Chapter Twenty-Eight
It's the Real Thing

The hotel had coffee, juice and doughnuts for us early birds. Our guide arrived and the four of us joined three other people in the green safari jeep. Actually, it wasn't a true jeep, but a spanking new pickup truck. Built into the open bed of the truck were three-tiered, cushioned bench seats. Overhead a canvas canopy protected us from the sun, and wooden panels on both sides kept us in and the animals out. As Amy once said, "This isn't Disney World, but the real thing!"

We weren't long inside Kruger Park when we saw our first animal—an elephant. It stood so still that I expected to see "Welcome to Kruger" printed across its body; much like a sign announcing you've entered the park. But when we saw the trunk move, we all gasped. Sure, I've seen an elephant before. Many times I watched this amazing animal walk back and forth behind the steel bars of a cage at the city zoo. But this was different—no bars separated us; no stacks of feed dished out on schedule; no caretakers. They were free and they were living in the wild. That's why seeing this elephant was a very exciting event. This was the real thing.

"Elephants form bachelor groups," our guide told us. "He will leave the herd until it is time to mate, and then he will return to the group." This one was definitely alone as he pulled branches off a single tree.

A short while later we bumped into Mei's favorite animal—the giraffe. There's something about giraffes; they're regal. "The male giraffe has thick horns while the female's horns are thin," our guide pointed out. "If you look closely you will see a bird taking a ride on the giraffe. This is a red-billed oxpecker and what it is doing is taking parasites off this animal. These birds can be found on many other animals."

"They're helping each other out," I noted. "The bird is removing ticks and the giraffe is providing food. That's really awesome."

"Does anyone know how long a giraffe sleeps each day?" the guide asked. Jerry, one of the other three people in the vehicle, guessed five hours. "No, not even close. The giraffe sleeps about 24 minutes each day and he does that standing up."

"No way!" we said as each of us shook our head in disbelief.

"Yes, 24 minutes."

"Is the giraffe the tallest animal?" I asked.

"Yes, but even though the giraffe is tall, it has only seven neck vertebrae which is the same as a human. There are special valves in his neck that prevent excessive blood pressure to its head when he stoops to drink. Now look over there. Do you see the leopard sleeping in the tree?"

"Where?" asked Dad.

"Look in the direction of two o'clock. There is a tree and the leopard is stretched out on one of the branches. Do you see it?"

"I see it," I said.

"Where, Shelly?" asked Mei.

"He's all slumped over and his paws are draped over the branch."

"I see it now!" Mei yelled out.

"The leopard is a nocturnal animal," our guide said. "Most of his activity is during the night."

We hadn't driven far when we saw this large bird in a tree with its wings stretched out. It had a spattering of white feathers on parts of its wings. Its goose-like neck had a reddish color on its underside. Its spear-like beak looked like it could do heavy damage to its prey. I asked the guide for its name.

"That's the African darter. He's holding his wings out to dry because his feathers are less waterproof than other water birds."

Soon we came across a herd of zebras. The guide said, "The zebra eats sweet grass. If you see the hair on its neck lying down, you know he is in a bad condition. If the hair on his neck is standing up, he is in a good condition. You can tell a male from a female by looking at the stripe on its backside. If the stripe is wide, it is a female. If the stripe is narrow, it is a male."

"A monkey's in that tree!" yelled Mei.

"Shh, Mei, not so loud," Mom said. "You have to whisper or you'll scare the animals away."

"Yes, talk with a quiet voice," the guide said. "The monkey you see is a vervet monkey. They spend most of their time hanging out in trees near rivers. They use these trees for their food and shelter. If you see this monkey raise his eyebrows, look out. That is often his way of showing aggression."

"He looks like he's sitting there wondering what we're staring at," Dad said.

Suddenly, our vehicle came to a stop. In front of us was a buffalo waiting to cross the road. The guide turned off the engine, and we patiently waited to see what he would do. He looked one way and then the other.

"I think he's doing the right, left, right rule of crossing a street," I said.

With some hesitation, he quickly made a move and bounded across the road. This scary-looking animal had one thick horn and a large, floppy ear on each side of his massive head.

The guide said, "Even though the buffalo is a feared animal, it is quite calm if not provoked. But it has a hot temper and can charge unexpectedly. It uses its curved horns to hook, toss, or gore its assailant and is considered a very dangerous animal." We all looked at each other with some apprehension.

"Hey, I see one of those birds on his head," Mei pointed out remembering to use a quieter voice.

The guide said, "Yes, that is the yellow-billed oxpecker. It is a cousin of the red-billed. Not only does this bird get its food from the buffalo by picking at ticks and larvae that hide in the buffalo's hide, but it receives a free ride. In return for that, the bird's chatter alerts the buffalo of approaching danger."

We continued to drive through the savanna. I saw very little color—mostly browns and yellows with an occasional green. "It is early spring but once summer arrives, your view would be obstructed due to the growth of leaves and brush," the guide said. "Let me talk about two trees—the marula and the baobab. The marula tree has a special fruit that is made into a liqueur, soap or lotion. Its nickname is 'Elephant Tree.' It is a very useful tree."

"I read a story about a baobab tree a long time ago," I said. "Isn't it kind of weird-looking? Almost looks like it has dreadlocks for branches."

"Yes," the guide said. "It has a boxy trunk with fat, stubby branches coming off the top. If you look over at the right, you will see one. I will stop the truck for you to take a look."

"The story I read was about this man who never cleaned out his car. It was so messy it had a baobab tree growing in the backseat. Eventually, he had to cut a hole in the roof for it to keep growing."

"Is that real, Shelly?"

"No, Mei, just a pretend story."

"On the left side of the road you will see a blue wildebeest," said the guide. "This animal is often seen with the antelope. They like to hang together."

"Why's that?" Mom asked.

"The antelope eats long grass while the blue wildebeest eats short grass. So they work together." When the wildebeest crossed over to the rest of the herd it joined several impalas. The impala looked like a deer with fawn-like colors; the top half being a dark brown while the bottom, a lighter camel color.

"Here's something for you to think about," the guide continued. "Do you see three dark stripes on the impala's backside? There is one stripe on each of his buns and a dark stripe on his tail. When the tail is down, it looks like an M. I say it is M as in McDonald's for the lion." Everyone laughed when we heard that. Our guide, always so serious, caught us off-guard with this joke.

We watched the blue wildebeest, impalas, and antelopes drink from the water hole. In a hushed voice the guide said, "If you look over by the water tower you will see a male lion."

"Yes, there it is," I said with much excitement.

"Everyone be still," cautioned the guide. "The other animals don't see the lion."

"I can see a second lion sitting under the tree," Dad said pointing over to the left.

Just then one of the wildebeest took note of the lions and started to run. Almost immediately the other animals followed, but then stopped frozen in their tracks never taking their eyes off the lions. The seconds seemed like minutes as the animals maintained their positions. I didn't know what I wanted to have happen. I knew lions prey on these animals. After all, that's the balance of nature. To see an actual kill would have been totally amazing and something perfectly natural. But I didn't want to witness any of those beautiful animals taken down. Soon the wildebeest, impalas, and antelopes took off once again only to stop a second time to check out the lions. Finally, one of the lions stood up, walked slowly over to a bush and hid in the tall grass. The other animals followed each other back to the water hole.

"I can't believe the animals are still there drinking water," I whispered. "I would've been so out of there." The guide started the vehicle and we slowly proceeded down the road. We were speechless and totally in awe after viewing that scenario.

Soon we ran into a kudu. "Look at his curly horns," our guide said. "Alongside his body are thin white vertical lines. Watch as he goes further into the bush. Do you see how he blends in with the brown dirt and the stick-like branches coming from the ground? He will gradually disappear from sight."

"You're right," Jerry's wife said. "The kudu vanished from my view finder as I tried taking a photo of him. Who knows where he went?"

"Anyone hungry?" asked the guide. "We are arriving at the park's center and you can grab something to eat. There is also a nice gift shop if you want to buy any souvenirs. I will park the truck here and give you ninety minutes. Is that enough time?"

We all agreed and took off for the concession stand. "Girls, here's the restroom," Mom said. "Let's go in there first."

We followed Mom in, but once inside, Mei yelled, "Shelly, Mom—look up! I looked up at the rattan ceiling only to find it covered with fruit bats.

"Oh, this is so gross!" I yelled. Even though their folded bodies hung upside down, I could see their tiny white eyes. It didn't matter that they slept; so many bats in one spot was like something out of a horror movie. We bolted out of there as fast as we could. After lunch we walked back to our truck. Mom opened the door and out jumped several monkeys. One of them had an apple in his hand while another held a half-eaten ham sandwich. The inside of our vehicle looked like a crime scene due to the pilfering that took place.

Our guide laughed and said, "They are little thieves. You are lucky they did not steal anything valuable." We cleaned everything up in the truck and climbed inside. But as we backed out of our parking spot, a monkey raced past us holding a blue water bottle in his mouth.

Back on the road we saw a black rhino. "Seeing this rhino means you have seen all of the Big Five," our guide said. "Does anyone know what the other Big Five are?"

"I do—the buffalo, elephant, lion, and leopard," I said remembering the Big Five animals Dad bought me at the V & A Mall.

"Good...getting back to the black rhino. This animal can be distinguished from the white rhino by its longer upper lip."

"Is the white rhino white?" asked Jerry.

"No, both rhinos are grey. They tend to show the color of the mud in which it rolls around."

"Why do they like to roll in mud?" asked Mei. "I wouldn't like having all that mud on me."

"It keeps the rhino cool," Dad explained.

"That is correct," said the guide. "It also cakes on the rhino's skin which helps suffocate ticks and prevents insects from laying eggs."

"Gross," said Mei as she scrunched up her face.

"Mei, you better be careful about the questions you ask. You may not like the answers," I teased.

We continued to drive through Kruger never tiring of seeing giraffes, elephants, and impalas. Ten minutes later our truck stopped and the guide said, "Look over there by the side of the road. Do you see a buffalo carcass?"

I spotted the remains of an animal with its bones and flesh sticking out from under a bush. "What do you think killed it?"

The guide pointed and said, "You will get your answer over there."

"I don't see anything."

"Look closely," the guide said. "Do you see a lion?"

"A lion!" we all said together.

"Oh, yeah, I see it now," said Mom. "Boy, I would've walked right by him and not even know it."

"There's another one!" Dad said. "Actually, I see a third lion and two cubs."

"Where?" I asked. "I don't see anything."

"Keep looking under that big bush."

"I see them now!"

When one of the lions stood up we saw just how massive his body was. The other lion remained in the grass under a tree. "Yes," the guide said, "those lions are waiting to finish their meal. It takes three male lions to take down a water buffalo."

Evening approached and our day on safari came to a close. Soon we were back on the paved road headed back to the hotel in Hazyview.

"How can we describe this day to people back home?" Mom asked.

"Impossible," said Dad, "absolutely impossible.

I nodded my head in agreement and said, "Hey, it was the real thing!"

Chapter Twenty-Nine
Guest Speaker

"Class, let me introduce Dr. Steven Kilpatrick, Shelly's father. He's here to share with us some of the issues he's working on at UCT."

"Thanks, Mrs. Van Wyk, for inviting me into your class. I understand you're studying about current global problems. Do any of you know what some of these major issues are in South Africa?" Several hands went up.

"How about the fellow sitting by the window?"

"Hi, I'm Jeremy. I know HIV is a big problem in our country."

"You're right. I can't overstate what a problem HIV is here. Almost one in five adults is infected. With special drug treatments, people diagnosed with HIV can lead relatively normal lives. The sad thing is few people have access to this treatment."

I glanced around and saw everyone listening to my dad

with a sense of seriousness. I wondered how many had someone close to them afflicted with AIDS.

"Dr. Kilpatrick, when did AIDS first exist in South Africa?" Sarah asked.

"Actually, the first recorded case of AIDS in South Africa was diagnosed in 1982 with the most rapid increase taking place between 1993 and 2000."

"Hi, Dr. Kilpatrick, my name is Robert. I always wondered why it took so long before anyone really did something
about AIDS." Robert, our class president, always appeared
on top of current events. He questioned things without making others uncomfortable. I guess that's why everyone liked
Robert.

"Well, Robert, your country found itself in the middle
of a major political change with South Africa focused on
its transition from apartheid. Unfortunately, during that time
HIV became widespread because it didn't get the attention it
deserved; at the very least, not acknowledged."

"Dr. Kilpatrick, Shannon here. My church went to a
small village near Johannesburg during our school recess last
December. We helped out a community of mainly orphaned
children. Some of them had one parent, usually a mother;
while most of the children were orphans due to HIV."

"Who was in charge of these children, Shannon?"

"There were adults living with them. Each family unit
had a small house consisting of two rooms."

"What did your church do?" Dad asked.

"Some people helped with farming. The village had a
huge garden that provided most of the vegetables the community needed. Others helped the community build an addition to the school."

"Did you help out?" asked my dad.

"Yes, I helped paint the inside of the old school."

"That's a generous way to spend your break, Shannon. I'm sure you returned with wonderful memories."

I looked over and saw Shannon smile as she nodded her head. I never really knew Shannon that well. Like Robert, she pretty much focused on school and spent little time socializing.

"Did you know Nelson Mandela's son died of AIDS in 2005?" Dad continued. "Mandela announced the cause of his death because he thought by doing so he would take away the stigma, and set the way for people to start treating it as a normal illness."

"Dr. Kilpatrick, I know another problem we have here," Jesse volunteered, "malaria."

"Yes, be especially careful of malaria in the summer when the insects are out. What do you kids do to prevent malaria? Shannon?"

"Spray with an insect repellent."

"Good...Don't forget to wear longer pants especially when you go into tall grass."

"We keep the doors and windows closed," Jeremy said.

"Isn't it the female mosquito that carries malaria?" asked Laura.

"Yes, the infected female carries germs in her saliva which then transfer to humans when bitten. These germs travel through the person's blood to the liver. The malaria results from a certain parasite that lives inside the liver and blood cells."

"That sounds nasty," yelled out Ben. I forewarned Dad about Ben, the jokester. Dad took his outburst pretty much in stride.

"You're right, it is pretty nasty," laughed Dad. "Currently, malaria is more of a threat in the northern part of South Africa. However, that could all change."

"How?" asked Shannon.

"Well, that leads us to the third issue facing South Africa as well as the rest of the world—global warming. That's the project I'm working on at the university. As temperatures rise, so do the numbers of people who are afflicted with infectious diseases. More provinces in South Africa could become malaria zones in fifty years. Not only that, the mosquitoes that carry malaria may spread to new places such as Scandinavia and the UK. Right now these countries are too cold to support these insects, but all that could eventually change if we aren't careful."

"Plant and animal species are in danger of being wiped out, too, due to climate change," said Robert.

"Definitely—in less than a century, thousands of plant species may be extinct, not to mention the reduction of bird and mammal populations. One thing we need to do is make sure there are wildlife corridors for all species to move and adapt to climate change."

"Are there specific places in South Africa that scientists are studying?" asked Robert.

"Yes, Robert, as a matter of fact there are," answered Dad. "About 1450 km northwest of here is one of the world's most threatened desert ecosystems—the Karoo. Its Mediterranean climate makes it possible to grow about 5000 different types of plants. Several of these are found nowhere else. Many of these plants are succulents. Do you all know what a succulent plant is?"

"I think they store water in their stems and leaves," volunteered Jeremy.

"That's right. With the possibility of a predicted twenty-five percent drop in winter rainfall and a two-degree rise in temperature, there could be devastating effects on the Karoo flora. The Karoo has become a lab for the study of this climatic impact."

"Dr. Kilpatrick, could you go into the affects of precipitation changes with the class?" asked Mrs. Van Wyk.

"Sure...the continent of Africa doesn't have the large mountain ranges that could provide water from snowmelt, rivers and precipitation. Most of the people living outside urban areas are reliant on surface water."

"My dad said that many Africans spend more time and money acquiring water than nearly any other natural resource," said Robert. "Is that true?"

"Sure is. Suppose there's an area that receives 600 millimeters of water. In America we'd measure that to be about 24 inches. If that precipitation dropped to 550 millimeters or 22 inches, how do you think that would affect the rivers? Anyone want to take a guess?" Ben was the only one who raised his hand. "Okay Ben, you want to take a stab at it?"

"Uh...I know... the water would go down." A few kids near the window laughed as Ben enjoyed his thirty seconds of celebrity. What he didn't realize is they were laughing at him and not with him.

Mrs. Van Wyk gave Ben a serious stare as Dad answered, "Well, you're right. The water level would go down." Three cheers for Dad in not missing a beat in spite of Ben's answer.

"Matter of fact," Dad continued, "the river drainage could drop up to 25 percent."

"That's one fourth of the river's water," Robert answered. "What about areas with little water to start?"

"People will do what they must to obtain it. You can't live without water."

"Less river water might create problems between countries," said Jesse.

"Great deduction," Dad answered. "There are many African rivers that cross international boundaries. And as the availability of water lessens, people go to where they can find it. Can you see how the migration of people could also set off massive conflict?"

"Which area of Africa would be the most affected?" asked Laura.

"With a ten percent drop in rainfall, parts of Botswana would be left with only a fourth of the surface water flow it currently has," answered Dad. "A twenty percent decrease might mean Botswana would completely dry up."

"How would the twenty percent decrease affect Cape Town?" asked Shannon.

"Cape Town would suffer a forty percent loss of its river water." Dad walked over to the map of Africa and pointed to the river systems. The length and width of many of the continent's rivers would dramatically shrink in size."

"Can this be stopped?" asked Shannon.

"First of all, Shannon, what's good is that government leaders have recognized this to be an issue to address. One idea being explored is to reduce the percentage of coal in South Africa's energy mix. Coal is the most abundant and cheapest energy source that energy plants use here. Coal power plants could be replaced with wind, solar or other energy sources that emit no carbon dioxide. Of course, vehicles that don't burn fossil fuel but instead run on electric or some other clean energy should be considered. But..." Dad paused and looked around the room, "with that said, South Africa produces less than two percent of all the carbon emissions in the world."

"This problem is everyone's problem," said Jesse.

Dad nodded his head. "You're right on the money, Jesse. It belongs to all of us."

Chapter Thirty
No Resolution

"Okay, everyone, we'll see you here shortly," Mom said as she started to sign off on the webcam. "Oh Stephanie, Shelly wants to talk to you."

I waited until everyone on both sides of the computer left and then said, "Hey Stephanie, what's happening?"

"Not much—just getting things together to come visit you guys. What's it like there?"

"Cape Town is a pretty cool place. I can't wait for you guys to visit at Christmas. My mom is coming up with some great stuff for us to do. You'll love the waterfront here."

"What do you do there?"

"Well, there are some awesome restaurants and even an aquarium. I like walking around the craft stalls. There are lots of things you don't find at home."

"Awesome—I can't believe you guys are having summer right now. It's so cold here," Stephanie said.

"I know. At first it was hard getting used to summer in December but I sure am adjusting to it. Did you know that instead of eating Christmas dinner inside, people here usually have a braai?"

"What's a braai?"

"That's what they call a barbecue in South Africa. There are lots of different words they use for things even though they're speaking English."

"Are you in any plays at your new school?" asked Stephanie.

"Last month the junior class put on *Les Miserables*. I was going to audition for a speaking part but decided to be part of the chorus instead."

"Why's that?" Stephanie asked.

"There were so many things to get adjusted to. I wanted to be part of the play because I thought that would help me meet some people, but I also didn't want to get too overloaded with work."

"Yeah, that's cool."

"Pretty soon I'll be facing finals and then I'll be a senior. It seems like I rocketed right through my junior year. We're talking fast forward—junior year in five months."

"How did you do that?" Stephanie asked.

"Trust me, it wasn't easy. Mom arranged for some extra tutoring which helped keep me afloat especially with Spanish."

"How's Mei?" Stephanie asked.

"Better now."

"She had a problem?"

"You remember how I worried about the move and Mei was excited? Well, wouldn't you know it was Mei who had some problems? There was nothing major. She just didn't have any neighborhood friends like she did back home. So Mom made a special point of inviting kids from her school over to play on weekends and things got better. I think she still misses Jennifer but at least she's not moping around."

"That's good to hear," said Stephanie. "Are you guys doing anything for Thanksgiving?"

"They don't have Thanksgiving here, but we're celebrating it on Sunday. Are you getting together at Grandma's?"

"We are. I'll miss not having you there to hang out with. Have you made any friends there?"

"I have. I met some really nice friends here. I think I told you about Laura."

"You did. She's the girl who was assigned to you on the first day to show you around."

"Yeah, that's the one. Then there's Kim. I look kind of short standing next to her. She's pretty cool."

"Oh, tall—does she play basketball?"

"No, she's into volleyball and she's really good. If I had to compare her to someone it would be Amy. She doesn't look like her but their personalities are similar."

"Who's the one that has the red hair?" Stephanie asked.

"Oh, that's Hannah. She has blasting red hair. It's so pretty but she hates it. She can be a little feisty at times, but that's what makes her Hannah. She came here from Ireland when she was ten. There are a lot of people here from other countries; like Laura was seven when her family came to Cape Town from Holland."

"Did Kim always live in Cape Town?" asked Stephanie.

"Yeah, and so did Lacey. Lacey is this person who's always smiling. She has this amazingly upbeat personality and can cheer me up whenever I need it. And lately, there've been times I've needed it."

"My mom told me about what that Trudy girl did to you."

"Yeah, she's definitely not a friend--public enemy number one. She makes Kylie Brezman look like a breath of fresh air."

"I remember you talking about Kylie, the girl from the play."

"Yep, the one and the same," I said. "Anyway, I heard Trudy is going to another school. It was such a big mess. I can't begin to tell you the problems she caused me."

"Why did she have it in for you?" Stephanie asked.

"It was like that from the moment I met her, Steph. Kim said she was jealous of me and never liked to have anyone else join their circle of friends."

"That is so mean," Stephanie said.

"I hate to say it but life has been so much better since she left. Oh, ya know, I better go and get ready for tonight. There's this function at school, and the girls will be here to pick me up. Looking forward to you guys coming."

"Yeah, it won't be long. See you soon, Shelly."

I logged off my computer and went to the closet to decide which jacket I should wear.

"Shelly, the girls are here."

"Okay, Mom...I'll be right there."

I ran outside to catch my ride. I could have walked but it's much more fun going with a group.

As I approached the car, I heard my mom ask, "So how does this slog thing work again?" I swear, she can be so embarrassing at times.

"Each class runs around the track from 4:00 till midnight to see which class can clock up the most laps," explained Laura.

"You're not running for eight hours, are you?" Mom asked. Oh yeah, totally embarrassing.

The girls laughed and Kim said, "No, we take turns. Our run starts at 6:00."

Mom looked at her watch and said, "Well, it's 5:00 now. I better let you girls go. Shelly, we'll be down at six to cheer you on."

"Sounds good," I said as I opened the back door of the car and climbed inside.

"Do you have your takkies *(running shoes),* Shelly?" asked Lacey.

"Right here in my backpack. Okay, let's go do this!" I said.

There were hundreds of kids as well as their families and friends at the school's track. Music played as we walked around the food stalls. I brought money for food, but Lacey suggested we eat after we run so we don't end up sick. We walked over to the table to check in when a flame thrower walked by.

"This looks like it's going to be a crazy time," I said to Laura.

"Shelly, don't look know, but here comes Trudy," warned Kim. The simple mention of her name got my heart pumping. "Just be cool, Shelly."

I tried to hide behind a large sign but she saw me.

"Well, if it isn't the snitch thinking she can come right in and take over," Trudy said in a snotty voice. I said nothing, signed in at the table and walked away. But Trudy followed me. "What's the matter? Are you too good for me?"

Ignoring her, I walked over to the bench and started putting my running shoes on. Trudy snubbed the other girls and immediately came over and stood in front of me. "Well, I think the snitch is afraid of me."

That was it. I was no longer able to remain silent. "You think I'm afraid of you? Ha! I just don't want to have anything to do with you. You're nothing but trouble. Now leave me alone."

"Hey, smart girl, I have a bone to pick with you. You got me expelled."

"I got YOU expelled! I believe the story goes that YOU got yourself expelled. If anyone should be ticked, it's ME!"

"Why don't you go back to where you came from?" Trudy screamed. By now a small group of people started to gather. I did not want the evening to play out this way. "Look, you troublemaker," she continued, "you've done nothing but create problems from the day you arrived."

"Trudy, you are so bizarre. Go away and leave me alone."

"Oh, little Miss Goody Girl wants to be left alone. I'll show you what alone feels like."

"Chips!" *(Watch out)* yelled Laura as she rushed over. Just as she stepped between us, Trudy raised her hand and struck Laura in the face. Laura fell to the ground and started crying. When Trudy realized that she struck Laura, she immediately bent over to help her get up.

"Trudy, what's the matter with you?" Laura cried. "You're acting crazy."

"Laura, I'm sorry. I didn't mean to hit *you*."

"You shouldn't hit anyone."

"Girls, what's going on?" I turned around to see Mr. Barratt, looking worried, rushing in our direction. "Laura, are you okay? What happened?"

Laura slowly sat up and looked at Trudy. "I don't know what's going on, Mr. Barratt. There seemed to be a fight brewing between Trudy and Shelly so I walked over hoping to stop it from happening. Next thing I knew, I was on the ground."

"Shelly, what's this about?" asked Mr. Barratt. For the next couple of minutes I tried to explain everything that happened.

"You're not going to believe all that crap, are you?" yelled Trudy.

"Trudy, exactly why is it you're on school property? You were told to stay away. I think you better come with me."

"I'm not going anywhere with you. I don't have to listen to all you stupid people," Trudy screamed as she took off toward the street.

"Come back here; this situation is not resolved," Mr. Barratt warned.

Trudy looked over her shoulder at us as she ran full speed between two parked cars. "As far as I'm concerned it is."

Then it happened. It happened so quickly that no one could stop it. First, we heard the loud screech coming from the brakes of a car; then there was a thud, followed almost simultaneously by an agonizing scream. For a few seconds I stood paralyzed and wondered if what I witnessed really took place or perhaps I was in the middle of an awful nightmare. A group of people close to the scene instantly raced over to Trudy. Confusion, panic, fear set in.

"Somebody, call an ambulance," a voice yelled out from the center of the mob.

Soon a lady rushed over and yelled, "Let me in. I'm a nurse." She managed to get through the mass of people and took Trudy's pulse. Instantly she gave her CPR and managed to stabilize her. I felt sick to my stomach as I stood at the rim of the crowd crying and shaking. Although everything happened so fast, the images I saw appeared in slow motion.

The ambulance arrived and took Trudy to the hospital. As I watched it speed away, my family came running over to me. I walked over to my mom and fell into her arms sobbing uncontrollably.

"Shelly, what's going on here?" Mom asked looking concerned.

"I didn't want any of this to happen," I cried, "but Trudy kept coming after me and wouldn't stop. And just as I turned to walk away, she lunged forward to hit me but instead hit Laura in the face."

"She hit Laura?" Mom asked in disbelief.

"Yes, Laura came over to stop her but got in the way. Then Mr. Barratt showed up and asked Trudy why she was on school property. He told her to come with him. Instead she took off running and was struck by that car."

The news of the accident quickly circulated throughout the crowd. My parents spoke with Mr. Barratt who suggested they take Laura and me home. As we explained to Laura's parents what had happened, she started to get a headache. Everyone agreed Laura should go to the clinic to get checked out to make sure everything was okay.

Later that evening, I sat quietly on the bench in my room and stared out the bay window into the dark night. Through the shadows I saw a cat run across the patio and slip into a bush. Probably running after a mouse, I thought. Everything appeared normal to the outside world, but it wasn't. How could such a fun day turn into something so awful? Why was Trudy so threatened by me? I never did anything to her. I decided I would swallow my pride and visit her tomorrow. Maybe we could work this situation out. It'll be hard but that's what needed to be done. I heard a soft tap on the door.

"Come in."

Both Mom and Dad entered my room and walked over to me. Mom sat down on the stool and asked, "How are you doing?"

"Not so good. I'm thinking about what happened today and what I could have done to prevent it."

"Shelly, I have something to tell you. Mr. Barratt just called. He said Trudy suffered massive head injuries from the accident and died two hours after arriving at the hospital. He wanted to make sure you knew that no one holds you responsible for what took place."

"Trudy died?" I asked totally in disbelief. "I didn't think she'd die. Couldn't they do anything for her?"

"Mr. Barratt said she suffered severe head trauma, and they were unable to record any brain activity at the hospital. After working on her for over an hour, her family decided to take her off the resuscitator. She passed away thirty minutes later."

"No! I don't understand why any of this had to happen." I fell to the floor and started to cry. My stomach felt nauseous as the room started to spin. "Why did she hate me so much? I wished I never came here. I want to go back home."

Mom sat down on the floor and hugged me hard. The night was silent. No one talked. Sometimes that's what needs to be done.

After a few minutes she said, "Shelly, listen to me. Mr. Barratt couldn't discuss the situation, but he did mention that Trudy was a troubled, young lady with lots of issues."

"Oh, Mom, I feel so awful. I told her to go away and leave me alone, but I didn't want her to die."

"Of course you didn't, honey. Trudy was behaving irrationally."

"I tried to ignore her. Maybe if...uh...I reasoned with her, she would still be alive."

"Shelly, you did what anyone in your shoes would have done. It sounded like Trudy was determined to pick a fight with you. You didn't want to get involved. That's certainly understandable," Dad said.

"Is Laura okay, Mom? Does she know?"

"Mr. Barratt said he called Laura's house to check on her and to let them know that Trudy didn't make it. I guess she's having a tough time with this also."

The doorbell rang and Dad left the room to answer it. A few minutes later I looked up and saw Laura by my door. Her swollen eyes partially concealed the nasty bruise over her right cheek bone. She walked over to me, and we immediately hugged each other as we let the heavy tears flow. Mom and Dad left the room allowing us the time and space to sort this out.

Chapter Thirty-One
Coming to Grips

A small girl dressed in a blue, two-piece bathing suit sat on a blanket stretched across the sand. She dug a hole with her shovel; then took off towards the Indian Ocean with her yellow bucket. As she dipped her feet in the chilly water, she shivered but didn't seem to mind. She filled her bucket, raced back to the hole, and dumped the water into it. Quickly the water disappeared.

A guy with a surfboard under his arm arrived. He wore a white baseball cap, turned backwards. Sitting directly on the sand, he stared at the waves—perhaps anticipating the adrenalin rush he would soon be experiencing.

Seconds later his buddy arrived, and the two raced toward the water foolishly thinking they could conquer the forces of nature. I watched as they jumped on their boards and let the water take them away.

Further on down, two brothers played catch—one

standing up while the other on his knees allowing himself to be the same height as the younger boy. Back and forth the ball traveled. Sometimes it found its way to the other's glove, but more often veered off in the direction of the water resulting in the younger child chasing after it. Neither boy appeared to tire of this pattern.

From a distance I saw a jogger wearing white shorts and a cap. He flew past two elderly women out for a morning stroll. They seemed a little startled at first, but soon smiled and nodded their heads at each other—gone were their jogging days.

Water is amazing. It's the place to be if ever I need to think. It doesn't have to be an ocean—a river or lake will do. Just being by it helps me sort out so many things. A month had passed since the accident and quite frankly, I can't free myself of the guilt. I knew I wasn't responsible for Trudy's death. Everyone kept telling me that, but somehow the pain that had taken root in the pit of my stomach just would not go away.

"Hey Shelly, why are you in a dwaal?" Startled, I turned around and saw Laura drop a blanket and beach bag onto the sand.

"A dwaal?" I asked.

"Yeah, you know—like in a daydream—a dwaal."

"Oh, some more of your African slang, I see. I'm just thinking about stuff, that's all. Here, let me help you with that blanket." I took a hold of one end of the blanket and stretched it across the sand. "Where are the others?"

"Kim and Lacey are on their way with the cooler," said Laura. "And Hannah had to go back to the car to get her sunscreen. She's not one to catch a tan. Looks like a great day for the beach."

"Perfect," I said.

"Here's the food," Lacey said as she placed the cooler down on a mat. "We brought drinks and sarmies (*sandwiches*) for everyone. Hey, check out the cute hottie slicing up the wave."

"Hottie?" I asked.

"Yeah, the surfer dude."

"Here I am." Hannah arrived sporting a tube of sun lotion. I smiled as I watched her methodically cover her limbs with the sun block. She glanced over at Lacey and said, "Boy, are you lucky you don't have to worry about getting sunburned. The sun can be evil to us redheads. And just look how my freckles are coming out— pop, pop, pop! Did you see that?"

Lacey laughed as she placed the snacks on one of the blankets. "You're just too much, girl." Hannah swiped her with a towel and then continued to cover her face with more lotion. She finished the ritual by wrapping herself in a blanket.

"Hey, it's almost summer. Why are you covering up?" Laura asked.

"Duh, what was it I just said—major sunburn is lurking inside those clouds."

Lacey took her sandals off and sat down next to me. "When are your relatives arriving, Shelly?"

"We pick them up at the airport tomorrow morning. I'm excited to see them."

"So it's your grandparents?" asked Hannah.

"Yeah, and my Aunt Carol, Uncle Charlie and cousin, Stephanie."

"Is Stephanie little?" asked Laura.

"No, she's actually a year older than us. She'll be graduating from high school in June."

"Kwaai! *(Excellent)* Will we get to meet her?" Kim asked plopping down on her towel.

"Definitely, you guys will have to come over while they're here. I know she wants to meet everyone."

"Where are all those people sleeping?" Kim asked stretching her long legs across the blanket.

"That took some figuring out," I laughed. "Mei is going on a cot in my parent's room. My aunt and uncle are getting Mei's room, and my grandparents will be in mine."

"Where are you going to be?" Laura asked. "You can sleep at my house if there's no room. My mom won't mind."

"Thanks, Laura. Actually, Stephanie and I will be on an airbed in the living room. It'll be crowded but it's only for twelve nights. At first we had the problem of where to put the Christmas tree. There was no room for it in the living room with us sleeping in there, but then my dad got the idea of setting it up on the back porch. So now we can open the drape, turn on the light, and presto—our tree!"

"That'll work," said Hannah.

"Yeah, especially with Christmas being in the summer," I laughed.

"Did you tell your family about Trudy?" asked Lacey.

"I told Stephanie the whole story last week when we were talking on the webcam. I think my mom told my grandmother about it."

"I'm sure their being here will help cheer you up," said Kim.

"Yeah, I can use some of that."

"I still can't believe Trudy's dead," said Lacey. "You know, we're all bummed out about this, Shelly. I don't know what got into her."

"I don't know why it bothered her so much having me come to Lesterford."

"It wasn't you, Shelly," Laura jumped in. "She was acting weird before you arrived."

"Yeah, I think it started around last January. She seemed moody; more than normal," said Kim.

"That's for sure," said Hannah. "I know I had to be careful or whatever I said would tick her off."

"What do you think was the problem?" I asked.

"Drugs," Laura said.

"Drugs? How do you know that?"

"I slept overnight at her house last April and she showed me her stash of marijuana. She also snuck prescription drugs from her mother. She wanted me to try some, but I told her I wasn't interested. Whenever she asked me to come over after that, I always made an excuse. So I think she felt threatened when she saw how quickly you fit into the group."

"And jealous," added Kim.

"Drugs will totally mess you up," said Hannah. "I know they changed Trudy."

"Did her parents know?" I asked.

"Probably, but I don't know for sure," said Laura. "I think they may have been in major denial."

"I'm glad you told me all this. I thought I brought this whole situation on."

"Actually Shelly, if there's anybody who should feel guilty, it's us," said Laura.

"What do you mean?"

"We knew about her problems but we did nothing. Maybe if we told her parents or someone at school, she could have been helped. You saw her shoplift and you told someone."

"Yeah, but I didn't right away. It's a hard thing to do.

I didn't want to get her into trouble. But then when I was dragged into this Spanish answer key mess, I had no choice. So you see, I was forced to tell someone."

"It's too bad her parents didn't get her the help she needed when that all took place," Hannah said resting her head on her beach bag.

"I don't think they did much of anything," Kim said covering her feet with sand.

"Yeah, instead they became very defensive," said Laura.

Hannah nodded her head in agreement. "Maybe they thought her problems would just disappear. You know, it's easier that way, thinking problems will take care of themselves."

"Girls, I'm glad we had this conversation. I've been pretty depressed about Trudy's accident. Never in my imagination did I expect anything like that to happen."

Laura stared out into the ocean and said, "Neither did we, Shelly."

Hannah stood up to get a drink from the cooler. "So you see, Shelly, you shouldn't feel like you're responsible because that's not how it happened. No more carrying that guilt on your shoulder. Hey, does anyone want a soda?"

"No, not for me," said Laura.

With that, everyone sat quietly watching the water; each person lost in her own private thoughts.

How lucky to have found this new group of friends. Never did I expect to have friendships like that here. As I thought back to how I worried about being alone in this faraway country, it suddenly dawned on me that my time in Cape Town was quickly passing. Amy was right. A year does go fast. How sad it'll be to say good-bye to these girls.

"OMG," Hannah yelled, startling everyone.

"What?" Laura asked.

"Have you seen my sun block? I'm burning up. Where's my hat? Ohhh, freckles…how disgusting. My arms are covered!"

Chapter Thirty-Two
Visitors from Home

"There they are!" yelled Mei. "Grandma and Grandpa! Shelly, there's Aunt Carol and Uncle Charlie!"

"Hi everybody," said Grandma as she hugged Mei, my parents and me. It's so good to see you. It's been five months. Give me a hug, Shelly."

"That had to be the longest plane ride I had ever been on," complained Aunt Carol. "We stopped in Dakar and had to switch planes to finish the flight to Cape Town."

"Yeah, I thought when we landed in Africa we were almost here," said Stephanie. Instead we had another eight hours to go."

"Turned out we were only halfway," joked Uncle Charlie. "I thought Steph here was going to jump out of her skin when she found that out."

"Well, let's get you guys to our place so you can freshen up," said Mom. "Are you hungry?"

"Are you kidding?" laughed Stephanie. "We had a lunch, two dinners, and three breakfasts flying here. Or was it two lunches and four breakfasts? I forgot."

Dad loaded the luggage into both of our cars. Seeing the situation, Uncle Charlie asked, "Will this be a problem, Steve? I can rent a car while we're here."

"No worries. Kathy and I each have our own car. No need to have three." Uncle Charlie, Grandpa and Mei got into Dad's car while Stephanie, Grandma, Aunt Carol and I got into Mom's.

"So tell us, Kathy, how do you like this place?" Aunt Carol asked as she sat up front next to Mom.

"We certainly miss home, but this city is a wonderful place to spend some time."

I sat straight up in my seat and said, "There's so much to do here, Aunt Carol. Mom has everything lined up. Stephanie, you'll have to visit the aquarium. There's one at the V & A that's really cool."

"What's V & A?" asked Stephanie.

"Oh, that stands for Victoria and Albert—it's the name of the waterfront."

"Shelly, you look like you've grown," said Grandma.

"I think I have. I've been getting those pains in my legs every once in awhile."

"Kathy, have you bought any diamonds?" Aunt Carol asked. "I heard this is the place to do that. I told Charlie that's what I wanted for my Christmas present, but he said coming here to see you was my gift!"

"I've never been a gift before," Mom said squeezing Aunt Carol's hand. "I'm so excited all of you are here. We're going to have so much fun. Oh, everyone, see that up there? That's Table Mountain," said Mom as she pointed out the window just as Dad did on our first day in Cape Town.

"Yeah, you can see it no matter where you are in the city," I said. "You guys want to go to the top?"

"How do you get up there?" asked Stephanie stretching her neck.

"Either walk or go by cable car. I recommend the cable car. It's pretty cool. You can see the whole city."

We were gabbing so much that before long we pulled into our driveway.

"Is this your place?" Grandma asked. "It's so nice."

"We like it. I do have to warn you that we'll be a little crowded. Shelly, did you tell Steph the two of you will be sleeping in the living room?"

"That's okay, Aunt Kathy, I don't mind."

"It'll be part of the adventure," said Aunt Carol as she looked at us and winked.

I swear this whole family is into adventures. Everyone spent the rest of the day drinking coffee, talking and taking naps. A "do-nothing" day was what our visitors requested.

The following morning we took a tour of Cape Town and then went up Table Mountain. This was no longer new to us, but showing the city to our family is what made the day special. Later that afternoon we drove over to the campus, and Dad gave a tour including the lab where he worked. Uncle Charlie seemed especially interested in Dad's work. Grandma enjoyed the beauty of the campus…the mountainous backdrop, the ivy covered buildings, and the stoned walkways with empty benches.

"Normally, this place is crowded with students, but with the school break it's pretty cleared out," said Dad.

Later that evening we went to the waterfront for seafood

at one of our favorite restaurants. "It's so weird eating out-side," said Aunt Carol. "At home we're up to our knees in snow."

"You came at a good time, that's for sure," said Dad. "This is South Africa's summer. I thought we could go to the aquarium tomorrow. Who's good for that?"

"Me," yelled Mei.

"Then we'll do it. The aquarium closes at 6:00 or we would go now, but we can come back tomorrow."

The following morning found the nine of us walking into the Two Oceans Aquarium. "Why do they call it Two Oceans?" asked Mei.

"Because Cape Town is between the Atlantic and Indian Oceans," Dad explained.

"Oh, I get it," said Mei. I loved how Mei always said that.

We got our tickets and went inside. The first exhibit had us tracing a stream from its mountain source to the ocean.

"This is really neat, Uncle Steve," said Stephanie.

"Yeah, Steph here is thinking of going into marine biol-ogy. She applied at the university and is waiting for an an-swer," said Uncle Charlie.

"She must have acquired your environmental interests," Aunt Carol said to Dad. We walked into the next room which had a glass tank that reached from the floor to the ceiling. Here we saw fish like Red Romans swimming. Next was the predator tank where yellowtails and ragged tooth sharks could be viewed.

"What's neat about this exhibit is that the tank is opened to the sea," Dad explained.

"What do ya mean?" I asked.

"As each tide comes in, fresh sea water is supplied to the fish inside."

"Cool...hey, what's that?"

"It looks like a touch pool," Mom said. "The sign says you can pick up the crabs, starfish, sea urchins, and the other sea creatures."

"Are they dead?" Mei asked.

"No, Mei," I answered. "You go for it, girl. I'll stand over here and watch."

Later that afternoon we returned to the car and Mom asked her usual question, "Mei, what did you like the best?"

"I liked the touch pool the best. But after that I liked the penguins. They were so cute."

"Did you know those penguins were actually rescued from oil spills?"

Aunt Carol turned to Stephanie and said, "This certainly was a great day, wouldn't you say, Steph?"

"I loved it! I dream about working at an aquarium like that someday."

"How about you, Shelly?" asked Aunt Carol. "Any dreams as to what you'll do after high school?"

"I have a few ideas floating around in my head. Right now I'm thinking of studying journalism at college."

"I didn't know you were interested in journalism," said Mom looking quite surprised. "How did you decide on that?"

"I like to write and...well...I found I really enjoy learning about other cultures. Then when we went to Robben Island and listened to the ex-prisoner speak about the apartheid, I discovered something about myself. I have a strong desire to search for answers."

Chapter Thirty-Three
Kirstenbosch

"What's that over there?" Stephanie asked as we passed a large arena.

"That's the rugby stadium," said Mom. "That place can hold up to 50,000 people. This area is called Newlands. We're actually in a suburb of Cape Town at the foot of Table Mountain's southern slope."

"Now why is this stadium here in Newlands and not right in the city?" asked Grandma.

"Good question—seems there's more space out here. Actually, Newlands is the headquarters for the Western Province rugby and cricket unions. Rugby is very popular here. People go crazy when the tri-nation teams play against each other," explained Mom.

"What's that?" asked Stephanie.

"The tri-nation teams are Australia, New Zealand, and South Africa," I explained. "Lots of times people will have friends over for a braai or a barbeque, and watch the game on TV. It's really a big thing."

"This seems like a nice place to live," said Grandma.

"We enjoy this area and getting into town is not a problem."

"Newlands also has lots of woods," Mei said. "Tell them about that, Mom."

Mom looked in the rear view mirror and smiled at her. "That's right, Mei. It's called Newlands Forest and soon we'll be driving right along that area."

"Follow Dad's car, Mom. It just turned," yelled Mei.

"I got it, Mei," said Mom. We pulled onto Rhodes Drive. "Now you can see the forests. Isn't it pretty up here?"

"It's nice they left this forest standing when they developed the city," Grandma said.

"I know. There are some fantastic, tall blue gums, eucalyptus, pines and silver trees. Often you can spot joggers or local residents walking their dogs. It's a very nice part of town."

"What's the name of this place we're going to, Mom?" I asked.

"It's Kirstenbosch Botanical Gardens, Shelly. We haven't been there, although we've driven by it a lot, so we'll be seeing it for the first time, too."

"Is that where the concert is?" asked Stephanie.

"Uh huh, every Sunday from November to April they have outdoor concerts. The gate opens at 3:30, but the concert doesn't start until 5:30, so that'll give us time to walk around."

Soon the nine of us were walking along the cobbled path towards the concert stage. On our way we passed several stone African statues. One in particular was a black African with a floppy hat and a ring through his nose. He held onto a large ball as he squatted amongst the trees and other green foliage.

"He looks like quite a character," Grandpa said.

Soon we arrived at the large, sandstone stage that had a white, acoustical ceiling. People were already filing in so Mom quickly pulled out two blankets and spread them on the grass. "This should secure our place on the lawn. Now, who wants to see the gardens?"

"I can't get over how well landscaped this place is," Grandpa said. "There's not a weed in sight." Dad pointed to a bench and told everybody to gather around it for a group photo. We found a guy who took a picture of us.

We continued over to the Useful Plants Garden. A sand-colored, circular hut with a thatched roof housed the many demonstrations. Scrubby plants surrounded this area. Labels that gave information as to how each plant could be used stood in front of the different shrubs and bushes. At first Mei tried to read all the labels but soon decided it was beyond her.

"What's this one say, Shell?"

I took a look at the sign and said, "Agathosma crenulata or better known as buchu. It says the San and Khoi people chewed these leaves to relieve stomach aches."

"Really? That's cool. What's this one called?"

"That's Artemisia afra—it's good for colds, coughs and flu."

"Now here's a familiar one," said Stephanie. "It's Aloe arborescens. Any guesses as to what this plant is used for?"

"Oh, aloe, that's for the skin," said Aunt Carol.

We continued to walk around the gardens until we came to a spot called Camphor Avenue. "This sign says that these camphor trees were planted by Cecil John Rhodes at the end of the 19th century," Mom read.

"There's that Cecil guy again," I said.

"You know, if you crush a leaf you can get a whiff of the unique camphor smell," Dad explained putting a crushed leaf to my nose.

"Let me try," said Mei. "That smells good."

"Is that Table Mountain over there?" Stephanie asked.

"It is," Dad answered. "Table Mountain can be seen from the gardens."

"What's in that building over there?" asked Mei.

"I believe that's the Conservatory," Dad said. "See the glass roof? It's a lot like a greenhouse. Let's go take a look inside."

We walked in and noticed this very weird tree in the center. "That's a baobab tree," I said to Steph. "We saw those on the safari. Don't you love how it looks?"

"It's so weird looking," Stephanie said scrunching up her face.

"I know, but that's what I like about it. Once you see one, you never forget it."

Inside the Conservatory were displays of all the floral regions of South Africa. There were plants from the coastal forest, the mountainous areas, the savannahs, and the desert regions. I looked at the sign and said, "See, the baobab is from the area near Johannesburg. That's where we saw it— at Kruger," I explained to Stephanie. It felt good to know something someone older and smarter didn't.

Soon we were at the gift shop near the entrance. We walked inside and spotted all kinds of books, African items, clothes made out of natural fibers, and gifts. Dad, Uncle Charlie and Grandpa sat outside on a bench while the rest of us had fun looking at all the merchandise.

Ride the Wave ~

"What do you think of this, Kathy?" Grandma asked as she held up a cream-colored placemat decorated with red protea flowers.

"I love it."

"I'm going to get a set of these. They should pack well."

Before long, Dad motioned for us to hurry. "The concert starts in 15 minutes."

Outside the shop Grandma said, "What a peaceful place, Steve."

"Well, enjoy the peacefulness because soon that'll change."

"What do you mean?" asked Grandpa.

"We never told you who'll be featured at today's concert. It's a popular South African rock group that won the South African Music Award last year."

"ROCK GROUP? I thought we'd be listening to some boring music," Stephanie whispered in my ear.

"Uh—me, too. Look!" I said pointing to a guy with spiked maroon hair, pierced nose and lip, and ripped jeans approaching center stage holding an acoustic guitar. "Things are looking up."

Chapter Thirty-Four
Cape of Good Hope

"I can't believe we're going home tomorrow," Aunt Carol said as she cleared the breakfast table. "This has been such a great vacation."

"I can't believe we have that long plane ride again," said Stephanie. We all laughed knowing that was definitely not Stephanie's favorite part of this whole trip.

"But today, no one is going anywhere but to the Cape of Good Hope," Dad said. "We're going to the very same spot Portuguese navigators explored looking for a sea route to India. So everyone get in the car."

I'll sit up front with you and Charlie, Grandpa said. "So, Steve, where did this big passenger van come from?"

"I borrowed it from this guy at work. He suggested I use it so we could all go to the Cape in one car."

"That was nice of him," Grandma said positioning herself in mid section with Mom and Aunt Carol. "Shelly, Stephanie and Mei, sit in the back. It's a lot easier for the three of you to crawl back there."

"How did the English get involved with this country?" Uncle Charlie asked as we pulled onto the highway.

"The way I understand it is the Cape was an area of conflict amongst the Dutch, British, and the Khoina people who originally lived here. At first, the Khoina eagerly participated desiring to be part of the trade opportunities, but things backfired on them."

"I can guess as to how that turned out," said Aunt Carol. "Look at the displacement of our own Native Americans."

"Look everyone, monkeys!" yelled Stephanie veering the conversation in a different direction. "They're in those trees!"

"Those are baboons," I said. "They run wild through these forests."

"Really? They're so cute."

"Don't let their cuteness fool you," Mom warned. "Baboons can be very dangerous." Dad parked the car in the parking lot and we climbed out of the van.

"You know," Stephanie said, "we learned about the Cape of Good Hope in school but it always seemed like a fairy tale kind of place. I guess I never thought about it as a real location with an actual environment." She pulled out her camera and took a picture of the piece of land that jutted out into the ocean.

From where I stood, it really didn't look like anything special. All over the ground were granular stones in between large rocks that washed up to shore. Kelp and other marine plant life were scattered around this barren area. After a few photos, we returned to the car. We drove over to Cape Point where we took a funicular to the lookout above. I walked over to where Dad stood. "The water is so blue. Is this where the two oceans meet?"

"No, that's a myth. They actually meet at Cape Agulhas. It's probably one of the world's most treacherous stretches of coast. Strong currents and heavy swells have sunk many a ship."

After several, group photo shots, we took the funicular back to the van and drove through the Nature Reserve. There we saw families of ostriches running wild along the coastline. Dad stopped the car, got out and returned with a stray ostrich feather for Mei. "Here you go, Mei. Next stop…lunch."

"Where are we eating, Steve?" Aunt Carol asked. "Is there a restaurant out here?"

"The same fellow who lent me this van recommended this place not far away. It's called the Black Marlin."

"Sounds like seafood," Aunt Carol said.

"Yeah, your first meal in South Africa was seafood, so we'll end the visit with seafood. The restaurant we're going to serves this fantastic skewered fish. I thought we should try it out."

"Okay, let's give it a shot," Uncle Charlie agreed.

We were hungry and anxious to get to the restaurant. No one talked but instead looked out at the beautiful African scenery that surrounded us in every direction. Suddenly, Stephanie broke the silence and gestured to a large wooden sign that stood by the road. "Hey guys, check out that sign."

Baboons are dangerous and attracted by food.

"We certainly know about that one, right Shelly?" asked Mom.

"No kidding." We then described the encounter with the group of monkeys on our safari in Kruger.

There were many people eating in the outdoor courtyard of the Black Marlin but we decided to eat inside. Everyone ordered the meal Dad suggested. As we waited for it to come, we heard a ruckus going on outside. I turned around and saw several waiters waving cloth napkins in the air. "What's going on?" I stood up and walked over to the door in time to see a group of baboons running along the crest of the roof. The largest one appeared to be the leader. He jumped off the roof and onto a table where several people ate. Everyone screamed as the baboon grabbed a dish of ice cream and ran off with it. Soon two baboons followed the leader and ran across another table. This resulted in everyone jumping up and running to the other side of the courtyard. Chaos was everywhere. The waiters managed to shoo these primates away, but by then everyone outside grew extremely anxious.

"Boy, did we make the right decision to eat inside," Grandpa said walking back to our table where the waiter had set a meal at each place. Cubes of King Clip were skewered with veggies in between to form a shish kabob. All of this hung vertically on a wroughed iron stand.

"This is a fantastic way to end our vacation," Grandma said. "Can't remember the last time I ate something this delicious."

"Yeah, tell your friend this was an excellent suggestion," said Aunt Carol.

"What time does your plane leave tomorrow, Grandma?" I asked.

"Around 9:15 in the morning but we have to be at the airport at least two hours before," Grandma said.

"No worries," said Dad. "I think if we leave the house

by 6:15 we'll be in great shape. Not much traffic on Sunday morning."

"So tell me, everyone, what was your favorite thing we did while you were here?" Mom asked as we dug into our food.

"Oh brother...here we go again." I mumbled.

"Now what's that suppose to mean?" Mom asked.

"You always ask us that question whenever we go some place," I complained as I raised my eyebrows.

"I noticed," laughed Stephanie.

"You two, stop picking on me. It's a good way to sum up what we've done."

"I agree. Kathy, I'll start," Aunt Carol volunteered. "Mine was the trip up Table Mountain. I enjoyed the view from the top. It gave a wonderful perspective as to where everything was located."

"I liked the botanical gardens," said Grandma. "What a wonderful day that was! The day after Christmas can be a little bit of a let down, but the gardens changed all that for me."

"I liked the gardens," said Grandpa. "I appreciated the amount of work that went into all that landscaping. What about you, Shelly?"

"That was my favorite day, too, except I have a different reason. The concert on the lawn was totally cool, especially since it ended up being a rock concert. No way did I ever think my parents would buy tickets to a rock concert."

"I liked the concert, too, but for me the best was the aquarium," said Stephanie. "It definitely was my personal favorite."

"Uncle Charlie, what was your favorite?" I asked.

"Hmm, I think it's right now. This meal is the best!"

"Charlie always judges things by food," laughed Aunt Carol.

"My favorite part was having you all come to visit," said Mom.

"We're so glad we did," said Aunt Carol. "This has been a truly amazing experience—a trip of a lifetime. Thank you for everything."

"I agree with Kathy," Dad said. "It's been our pleasure having you here. You cured a few good cases of homesickness by coming."

Mei clicked her glass with her fork. "What about me? No one asked me what my favorite thing was."

"Mei, you're next," said Aunt Carol. "Tell us, what was your favorite part?"

"Christmas!"

Chapter Thirty-Five
New Beginnings

"**Y**our family's nice," said Laura as we walked over to the tennis courts after our first day back to school. "I'm glad I got to meet them."

"Thanks, we had a great time showing them around. The vacation went by so fast. Ya know, it's an adjustment starting a new grade level in mid January. It seems so weird to me."

"But Shelly, it makes sense. It's a brand new year. I think what you do is weird—starting a new level in September. So, tell me, how's that going to work when you return home?"

"I registered for a couple of half year courses this semester—like political science, art, and creative writing. They'll be completed by the time I return. I'm also starting physics. I heard it's hard, so this way when I restart my senior year at my other school, I'll have a pretty good headstart. At least that's how I'm looking at it. I'll also continue with Spanish. Hopefully, I'll get a better handle on it."

"Do you plan on restarting your senior year in September?"

"Yeah, I want to graduate with my friends. I decided I wasn't in any hurry to finish high school. Besides, to finish here would mean I would need to stay until the end of November and that's not possible."

"What do you want to study when you go to the university?" asked Laura.

"I'm thinking maybe journalism. I see myself reporting the news on CNN," I laughed. "Oh well, everyone needs to have a goal and that one's mine…at least for now. What about you, Laura?"

"I want to get my bachelor's degree in nursing and then go on to be a nurse practitioner. There's a real need for nurses in our country."

"I see you doing that. Where will you go, UCT?"

"Actually, I'm thinking of going to Holland to study. I'll probably stay with my aunt and uncle who live there."

"You were little when you came here, right?"

"I was seven but we've been back to visit a few times."

"Do they still wear wooden shoes?" I asked half-teasingly.

"Yeah, just like Americans wear cowboy boots and hats."

"That's not a joke; many people in places like Montana and Texas do. Someday you'll have to come and visit me. But I have to tell you, Laura, I live far from Texas."

"I would really like to do that," Laura said as we left the covered walkway that led from the Science building to the tennis courts. "Darn, looks like the courts are filled. Let's check out how long of a wait it is."

We were walking along the fence when we spotted two guys getting on the last available court. One waved and yelled out to us.

"Shelly," whispered Laura, "there's Kevin Brodie and Spencer Butler playing on court five. Hi guys!"

"I know Spencer from the play but I don't know Kevin," I whispered back.

"Great rugby player—he's gorgeous, don't you think?" asked Laura.

"Yeah, you're right about that." I took a deep breath as I checked out this tall guy with blonde curly hair.

"Hey girls, want to play some mixed doubles?" yelled Spencer.

"Sure...looks like all the courts are taken," said Laura. "You guys know Shelly? She's here from America."

"No, I don't think we met," said Kevin. "Where in the states are you from?"

"New York," I answered.

"Fantastic city," Kevin replied. "I went to the United States two years ago and we landed in New York."

"Yeah, it's certainly not like any other city around. But actually, I live about three hours away from the city in a small town. People are always getting the city of New York mixed up with the state," I laughed. Kevin smiled at me and I felt the blood start to rise in my head.

We tossed to see who would be partners and I ended up with Spencer. Probably a good thing as I don't know if I could concentrate playing next to Kevin.

At the end of three games the guys asked if we wanted to get something to drink. Crazy question that was! "You girls have a jammie here?" Spence inquired.

"A jammie?" I asked. "What's that?"

"That's slang for car," laughed Laura. "We've been helping Shelly with her South African English."

"I see," said Spencer nodding his head in agreement.

"Actually, we walked. We live close by," Laura explained. We got into Spencer's car and headed for a snack shop not far from school. It was awkward deciding where everyone should sit, so Laura and I shoved into a booth opposite each other, letting the guys decide that. My heart pounded as Kevin slid next to me. I noted this moment—definitely a headliner in my email to Amy.

After everyone ordered slap chips *(French fries)* and cokes, the conversation went from what brought me to Cape Town; drifted to my first safari experience; and finally, the accident involving Trudy.

"You definitely should not feel responsible for the accident," said Kevin in a sympathetic voice. "I heard she had some major issues."

"Yeah, I know. Tell me, Kevin, have you always lived in Cape Town?" I asked trying to change the subject.

"Uh huh, born and raised here. My grandparents were imports," Kevin laughed.

"From where?"

"Holland," he answered.

"Oh, like Laura."

"My grandfather came over quite a few years ago and opened a pharmacy in Constantia. My dad runs it now."

"Is your dad a pharmacist?" I asked.

"He is."

"I have a friend back in the states whose mother is a pharmacist."

"Really? That's what I plan to study when I go to the university."

"Will you work for your dad?"

"He would like that, but I'm not sure I want to live here.

I'd really like to live in America but my parents aren't too happy about that idea."

"Why?" I asked.

"They say it's too far away."

After we left the restaurant and returned to the car, Kevin and Spence asked us if we wanted to go to the movies on Friday. I looked over at Laura and gave her a pleading look. She understood and said, "That sounds great. What time?"

"We'll give you girls a call back as soon as we check out the schedule," said Kevin. We gave them the directions to where we live, and I was dropped off first. I got out of the car, waved good-bye, and flew into the house.

"Hello family," I yelled.

Dad greeted me at the door. "What are you so up about?"

"I had a fantastic game of tennis and the best coke and slap chips ever! Life is s-o-o good!" I yelled over my shoulder as I flew into my room and shut the door.

"Did she say slap chips? What in the world are slap chips?" Mom asked.

"Don't know. But the girl is up…enjoy the moment," Dad answered shrugging his shoulders.

Once in my room, I threw off my shoes, tossed my tennis racket onto the bed, and turned on the computer.

Hi Amy,

Wait until you hear about my day! Laura and I met up with two very cute guys after school today. One of them…Kevin…is especially cool. I mean eons over Josh Zettleman. Want to know an awesome thing about him? He doesn't even know he's cool. Hey, what would you think if I said tennis may be my sport of choice?

Chapter Thirty-Six
One of a Kind

Lacey Nkumba had become a close friend. She's always lived in Cape Town. Actually, she told me that as a young man her father lived in a shanty town in Durbin, but moved to Cape Town before she was born.

"My dad said there were better opportunities for him here. My grandmother always encouraged my dad to stay in school and get as much education as he could. He became the first person in my family to graduate from school."

"What did your dad do after that?" I asked as we walked to the art room.

"After high school he worked as a doorman at a hotel in Durbin," said Lacey. "He was a hard worker and that caught the attention of the owner of the hotel chain who would visit every few months. One day this man told my father he would pay for his education at the university to study hotel administration. In return, my father would agree to stay with the hotel organization for at least five years after he graduated."

"Wow, this guy must've really liked your dad," I said.

"Yes, my father told me this was a special blessing."

"Were you born yet?"

"No, my father met my mother in college. After graduation, he and my mother were married."

"So how did he get to Cape Town?" I asked.

"He worked in the hotel's office in Durbin a few years until he became the manager. Several years later he was transferred to Cape Town to open a new hotel. That was when I was born."

"That's an amazing story, Lacey."

"My father said the owner told him one day he should repay the favor by helping someone else improve on their situation."

We walked into the art room and spotted our art teacher, Mr. McKune, talking to the guest he invited to speak to our class.

"So enough about me, how long have you and Kevin been going out?" asked Lacey as we sat down waiting for class to begin.

"We're not really going out. Actually, I don't know what it is we are. We've had five or six dates and we talk on the phone a lot. I'm getting very confused about this though," I said looking around, making sure no one overheard our conversation.

"Don't be confused," laughed Lacey. "Just enjoy the ride!"

"That I'm doing," I said with a nervous giggle. "But the problem is I'm beginning to really like him, and here I'm leaving in July. Don't mention any of this to anyone, okay?"

"No problem about that. Shh...here comes Mr. McKune. We'll talk later."

At that moment the bell rang and Mr. McKune announced, "I want to welcome our guest speaker, Mr. Shilowa, to our class. Mr. Shilowa is an artist who is part of the production crew for Raku. I asked him if he would come to class and explain how this art work is produced and he accepted the invitation. So I would like you to help me welcome Mr. Shilowa."

"Thank you, Mr. McKune, for the invitation. I always enjoy speaking to budding artists about what it is we do. Before I begin, let me ask how many of you know about Raku?"

Everyone but me raised their hand. I had no idea what Raku was.

"Yes, I see most of you have seen this type of craft in the markets, yes? Actually, Raku is a type of earthenware originally used in Japanese tea ceremonies. Today we use this process to make other things like animals—giraffes, elephants, zebras, hippos—animals like that found in Africa. I've come today to tell you the steps we take to make these colorful animals. There are many steps in this process," Mr. Shilowa continued. "First, a designer makes a solid mold. Then a working mold used for production is made from the original one. Here is an example of such a mold. Any questions so far?"

I raised my hand and asked, "Do you use clay?"

"Yes, good question. These are press molds. After we press the clay and take it from the mold, we remove all excess clay and smooth out the animal. Someone then etches a pattern in the animal. Have you ever done that?"

Several of us nodded our heads. "I did that with harden

bread dough when I was a kid," said this one girl in the back of the room.

"You start young, you get to be good at this," Mr. Shilowa said. "You come work at the factory." Everybody laughed as Mr. Shilowa displayed a huge grin.

"Now, next step…after the clay has dried out we put the figure into a kiln for the first firing. This is called the bisque firing. Anyone want to guess for how long we keep it in the kiln?"

"I think it's for a day," answered Shannon who sat behind me.

"You're right! It fires in an electric kiln for 12 hours and then another 12 hours waiting for the kiln to cool down. Temperatures get to 1000 degrees Celsius. Now it is called bisqueware." Mr. Shilowa went over to the table and raised an example of an elephant bisqueware for all of us to see. "I will pass this around so you can see it up close. Next, it goes to the painters. They use Raku glaze to hand-paint the figure using very small brushes. Any idea what happens to it next?"

Lacey raised her hand and said, "In ceramics after it's painted we put it back in the kiln."

Mr. Shilowa nodded his head. "Same thing here. The difference for Raku is the second firing takes place in a gas kiln unlike the electric one used in the first firing."

"Is it heated to 1000 degrees again?" Shannon asked.

"No, a little cooler…950 degrees Celsius…and for not as long either. It's inside the kiln for about 20 minutes. The top of the kiln is removed and when the red hot clay body comes into contact with the much cooler air, the glaze cracks. While the items are still very hot, they are transferred to a drum of sawdust where they smolder. This makes smoke which gets into the fine cracks of the glaze that were created a few moments before. Here's a giraffe showing how the smoke blackened not only the cracks but also the unglazed surfaces. Then the items are removed to cool down further. Someone washes it and finally it's inspected to make sure it is of the best quality."

After class I walked out of the room to find Kevin waiting for me. "Hey, want to play some tennis?" he asked.

"Sure, but first come and see this."

He followed me back into the art room where I pointed out several of the animals still on display. Their varied colors positioned as horizontal blocks on the animals were unique. "Isn't this awesome? My favorite is the elephant."

"Oh, Raku—yeah, it's pretty cool stuff."

"You know about it?" I asked. "I just love it. I can't get over how such a simple process can result in something so special."

"You can find this stuff in a lot of the gift shops around here," said Kevin. "It's pretty pricey."

"Mr. Shilowa said…"

"Who's Mr. Shilowa?" asked Kevin.

"Oh sorry, he's that guy over there. He came to our class to explain the steps of how Raku is made. He said that every person who works on a piece will either etch or paint their initials on the bottom of the animal." I turned a finished elephant upside down. "See? There are about eight sets of initials. It's truly one of a kind."

Kevin grinned and poked me in the side. "You're one of a kind. C'mon, let's play some tennis."

Chapter Thirty-Seven
Garden Route

"Hi everyone," I said waving to Amy, Natalie and Erin who were waving back on the computer monitor."

"Hey, what's happening?" Natalie asked.

"I just finished my term so we have a week off," I answered.

"It's weird how school is different over there," said Amy.

"Mostly with the scheduling," I said. "You know, the seasons are the opposite so the schools here start and finish at different times. It took some getting use to, and I don't think I'm really adjusted to it even now."

"When do you come back?" asked Erin.

"My dad won't be returning until August, but my mom decided the three of us would leave in July. The half year courses I'm taking will be over in June."

"Have you had any time off?" asked Erin.

"Only one week here and two weeks there," I answered. "I'm excited about coming home and having some decent time off before I begin my senior year AGAIN. It's confusing and weird but somehow we have it all figured out."

"We really miss you, Shelly," said Amy.

"Thanks, guys, same here. But you know, the year is going fast. I made some great friends here and really wish I could take them back home so you guys could meet them. They've heard so much about you."

"Are you still going out with that Kevin guy?" asked Natalie.

"I am. He's such a nice guy—not at all stuck on himself. He certainly could be."

"How's that going to work when you have to leave?" asked Natalie.

"I don't know, Natalie, I really don't. It's going to be tough saying good-bye in a few months. My mom warned me about that when I first started dating him."

"You know, Shell, if you were dating him here it would be pretty much the same thing," said Erin.

"What do you mean?" I asked.

"Well, you guys would be saying good-bye and going off to college."

"I guess you're right, Erin. I never thought of it that way."

"Why do you like him so much?" asked Amy. "Is he really cute?"

"He is but it's more than that. He's just such a nice person, ya know, not a jerk. We really have a good time together. And he's so smart. He's been helping me with my physics lab reports. I started taking physics this year hoping to get a handle on it."

"Why did you do that?" Amy asked. "You'll be taking it next September at Jackson."

"I just thought getting a head start might make it easier for me in September."

"Are you still playing tennis?" asked Natalie.

"I am and I'm improving, so you better watch out because I might whip your butt!"

"Do you play a lot?" asked Amy.

"Pretty much…Kevin and I play quite a bit and the practice is starting to show. Would you believe I just might join the tennis team at Jackson?"

"OMG, Shelly on a sports team," laughed Amy.

"Yeah, who would have thunk that?" I asked.

"Have you been taking anymore trips?" asked Erin.

"Actually, we're taking off to do this thing called the Garden Route. This is our last chance to do some serious traveling while over here. My mom really wants to go there."

"And you don't?" asked Erin.

"I do and I don't."

"Does Kevin have anything to do with the don't part?" Amy asked.

"You're reading me," I laughed. "My parents told me I could invite Laura."

"Oh, that's their way of getting you happy to go," Natalie said.

"I know. I figured them out."

"Not much going on here," Erin said. "Most of the talk is about the Junior Prom, dresses, who's going with whom… that kind of stuff."

"I can't believe it's been a year since I went to the prom with…what's his name? ha ha."

"Yeah, a lot has happened since then," said Natalie.

"Well girls, I better sign off. Something seems to be going on in the kitchen with Mei. Keep me posted on the Junior Prom."

"Bye!" everyone yelled.

After shutting down the computer, I walked into the kitchen just in time to witness Mei having a meltdown. "Hey, what's going on here?"

"Don't stare at me!" Mei yelled.

I looked over at my mother who shrugged her shoulders and gave me a look that definitely meant to keep quiet.

"I don't see why Shelly can take a friend and I can't. It's not fair," cried Mei.

No question about it, Mei was entering a phase. I saw it begin right after Christmas and it appeared to worsen as each month went by.

"Mei, Shelly's a lot older," Mom explained. "At your age she didn't take a friend along on a trip either. So you can either make yourself miserable or you can accept it." I recognized this little speech—the old swim along with the wave spiel. I almost told Mei to give up on this one as she won't win, but decided to keep my mouth shut. I certainly didn't want to jeopardize Laura coming along with us. No, I'll go outside and mind my own business.

After dinner Laura came over to the house to sleep since we were leaving early in the morning. "What's with Mei?" she asked.

"Don't take offense but she's mad because you're going and she can't take a friend."

"Want me to say something to her? Would that help?"

"Probably not—best to just pretend you don't notice. My mom told me to include her in things. That should make for a lekker time!" I chuckled to myself realizing I picked up some of the South African slang.

The next morning we lugged our things into the back of the car. "I can't believe how much you girls pack for only a few days," Dad complained. "I have one small duffel bag."

Our first stop along Route N2 was Swellendam which turned out to be a very picturesque town. Later we learned it was founded in the mid 1700's by the Dutch.

"It seems like every time I learn something about this country the Dutch are involved," I told Laura as we got out of the car.

"We're all over the place. See that church with the tall clock tower? I remember going into that church when I was here with my family several years ago. Check out the hills behind it. Is that cool or what?"

"They look like elephant legs," I said stopping to take a picture with my camera. "Stand over there, Laura. I'll get you in front of that tree."

"Girls, we're heading over to the Drostdy Museum," Mom said coming up behind me. "Isn't this the cutest town?"

"What's the Drostdy Museum?" I asked.

"It was first used as the seat of the magistrate back when the Dutch East India Company built it," said Dad. "Today it's a museum." We walked along the sidewalk until we came upon a whitewashed Dutch cottage with a thatched roof and shuttered windows. There was a stone courtyard in the front of the building, and at the entrance three musicians greeted us with jazzy tunes. One guy played a sax, the second had a guitar, and the third fellow strummed a banjo. After listening for a little while we went inside to take a look. What we saw was an example of how a home during the 18th century once looked. As I looked at the old furniture and art, I tried to imagine what it would be like living here during colonial times. We left the building and right outside the front door I noticed an oval shaped pool. Inside the lily pads sprouted blooms of white flowers. I stepped up onto the small stoned wall that surrounded the pool when I spotted Mei on the opposite side kneeling over trying to smell one of the flowers. She looked so cute that I decided to take a photo of her.

"Be careful there, Mei," Mom warned.

"I'm hungry. Can we eat soon?" Mei asked.

"That's the plan," Dad answered. "There's supposed to be a nice restaurant just up the road." We walked over to another white building that used to be someone's house. It had a friendly looking covered porch with a big sign hanging in front that said RESTAURANT. We walked up the porch steps and sat down at one of the many tables lined up on the porch.

"I'll have a hamburger," said Mei.

"They don't have a menu, Mei," said Mom. "Lunch is served family style."

"What's that?" Mei asked hopping up on a chair near the front door.

"It's like what you would get if we ate at home. Large platters of food are brought out for everyone at the table to share," answered Mom.

After lunch we returned to the car and headed out toward Mossel Bay where Bartolomeu Dias became the first European to land in South Africa. We went to the Bartolomeu Dias Museum to see a full-sized replica of his ship.

"This isn't the real ship," Dad said. "This one is a replica."

"Where did it come from, Daddy?" asked Mei.

"The sign says it was built in Portugal in 1987. They actually sailed it to Mossel Bay, lifted it from the water and lowered it into the museum."

"How did they do that?" I asked.

"They made alterations in the roof and built a sunken floor to house the keel."

"That's awesome," I said as I checked out the pulleys, ropes, rudder and the red cross displayed on one of the sails.

Once we were outside, Dad said, "Take a look at this tree."

He pointed out a gnarly old milkwood next to the museum. "Back in the 16th century seafarers left messages for each other in a shoe that suspended from a tree like this one."

"That's weird," I said while taking a photo of it.

"Yeah, it's called the Post Office Tree. Well, I think we're done here. Let's get back in the car and do our own exploring." As we drove by the ocean we could see bench swings facing the water. After we passed a lighthouse, Dad parked the car, and we walked along a path at Mossel Bay that wound its way to the top of a crag.

"Girls, look over there," Dad whispered. He pointed to a hollow in the rock.

"Oh, those are dassies," Laura said.

"What in the world are dassies?" I asked as I watched these weird looking creatures dart from place to place. "They kinda look like small groundhogs."

"Yeah, but they aren't. Their real name is rock hyrax. Can you believe they're relatives of the elephant?" Laura said.

"No way! They're so small."

"Laura's right," said Dad. "They have tusks but they're

located inside their mouth instead of extended like the elephant's. Besides that, their internal organs and skeleton closely resembles an elephant's."

Laura walked around three dassies that scampered under a rocky overhang. "Mei, here's something else. You know how we have one stomach? Well, a dassie has four."

"No it doesn't," said Mei, "you're fooling me."

"No she's not, Mei," said Dad. "It does—strange animal, don't you think?" We returned to the car and pulled back onto the highway.

"Is that wheat growing in that field?" Mom asked Dad looking out the side window.

"Yeah, the farmers are having a great year due to the rainfall and they deserve it. The past several years this area suffered from a drought and nothing grew."

"What's that smell?" asked Mei.

"You're smelling gas," Dad said. "There are oil refineries outside of Mossel Bay."

"It sure stinks," Mei yelled pulling her jacket over her head. Outside I saw shacks alongside the road. I couldn't help but notice how they contrasted with the condos, large hotels, and chalets we saw in Mossel Bay.

"Where are we going next?" I asked.

"Our next stop will be Wilderness. We're going to check into a hotel and stay there for a couple of days," Mom answered. "We should be arriving soon."

I paid little attention to the conversation as I continued to look at the rows of shanty towns consisting of cinderblock or concrete cottages. Each one had a tin roof painted pink, white or robin's egg blue. Some of the shacks were either falling down or staked up with 2 x 4s. Clotheslines hung between the houses and stick fences marked off boundaries. Every so often I saw a water faucet in the middle of a communal area where people collected their water. A little further down the road, what appeared to be an invisible line of demarcation, marked the end of the shanties and the start of the government built homes. These houses were simple, but of a sturdier construction.. Eventually, all of the shanties would be torn down and replaced with these homes.

Beautiful mountains often hidden by puffy clouds surrounded this area. Shrubs, clusters of trees, brownish grass with sprouts of green and purple heather finished the picture. The land extended as far as the eye could see only to be interrupted by an occasional hill or bridge.

"Was there a fire here?" I asked as we passed a scorched field with tree stumps next to untouched grass.

"What you're seeing is the result of controlled burning. This is done to replace nutrients into the soil and to keep fires from destroying acres of land," explained Dad.

Everywhere on the highway I saw telephone poles strung together with wires and more wires. Soon the Indian Ocean peeked between the rolling hills. Upscale residences strategically placed for an ocean front view could now be spotted. Some were constructed of stucco, a few from logs, but many were built of brick. What they all had in common was the Mediterranean styled, red tiled roofs.

"Look at that view over there." Mom pointed to a steep grassy hill with the silhouette of one lone tree stretching its branches against the purple African sky.

"Now that's a great picture," Dad said as he drove the car to the side of the road. Mom jumped out, took her prize winning shot, and climbed back into the car. We continued the journey as camel-colored fields and recently planted rows of maize and hops flashed by the window. A continuous string of bridges crossed over a series of rivers with the water from each eventually feeding into the Indian Ocean. The view was stark yet unbelievably beautiful. Soon our car pulled off the highway. We had arrived in Wilderness.

Chapter Thirty-Eight
A New Concern

"What did you do last week?" I asked Kevin as we sat down on a bench located in the outside courtyard of the school.

"Not a whole lot. Wished you were around. I missed you."

I looked away as I felt my face flush. Feeling uneasy and not knowing where to go with it, I chose to ignore his comment. Instead I said, "We had a great trip. I saw lots of stuff but the best was the Featherbed Nature Reserve."

"Did you do the hike?"

"Yeah, it was cool."

"Did you go from the Heads?" asked Kevin.

"What's that?"

"They're these two sandstone cliffs that protect the lagoon."

"That sounds about right. Are they in Knysna?" I asked.

"Yeah, you would connect with the ferry from there," said Kevin.

I nodded my head. "We did the ferry, then took a tram up to the top of Featherbed and hiked down. At one point we were so high the motor boats looked like matchboxes."

"I've been there several times," said Kevin. "It's a fantastic hike."

"I thought the force of the waves hitting the big rocks was awesome. But the funniest thing was this big white sign with large blue letters that said, 'Is there life after death? Trespass here and find out.'"

Kevin laughed. "Yeah, I know the sign. Did it have a drawing of a skull and bones?"

"The same one," I answered glancing at my watch. "I better get inside. My class starts soon. See you at lunch?"

"Not today, I have to go to the weight room. How about after school? I'll give you a lift home."

"Sure," I said. "Meet you in the parking lot." I waved good-bye as I opened the door to my writing class. I walked inside and took my seat next to Hannah.

"Hi Shelly, I talked to Laura last night and she said you guys had a great time."

"We did."

"I saw Kevin hanging with his friends. He looked miserable."

"Really? He said he missed me while I was in Wilderness. It was weird and awkward. I didn't know what to say."

"Why's that?" Hannah asked.

"You know, I'm leaving in a couple of months for good."

"And the point is?"

"The point is that I never thought I'd be this upset to leave. Actually, I thought I would hate it here."

"You did?"

"I guess that didn't come out right! No offense, but when I first heard we were moving to Cape Town, I didn't want to leave my friends back home. You see, I didn't know this place would be so cool. I do miss my other friends, especially Amy. But then there's you, Laura, Lacey, and Kim."

Hannah smiled and said, "And Kevin—let's not forget Kevin."

"Yeah, and then there's Kevin."

"How's that going to work?" Hannah asked.

"I don't know. It's not going to be good."

Mrs. Wellington walked in and closed the door. "We'll talk later," Hannah said as we turned our attention to the front of the room.

All that day a raw feeling took root in the pit of my stomach. I found it hard to concentrate but I knew I had to. As I waited in the parking lot at the end of the day, I thought about Kevin and how a short four months ago I never knew he existed. I knew I would be leaving and so did he. I wondered if it bothered him, too.

"BOO!"

"Ahhh! Kevin, you scared me!" He laughed as he unlocked the car door and I got in. I think it's hard for guys not to tease—seems to be part of their nature.

"What were you thinking about?" he asked starting up the car. "You seemed to be in another place."

"Oh, nothing much…just stuff."

"Stuff? Like what kind of stuff?" Kevin said pulling the car onto the road. "Uh oh, something's wrong. What's up?"

"We never really talked about this but…you know…I'll be returning to New York in July."

"I've thought about it a lot," said Kevin as he looked

over at me. "Hey, let's not have that keep us from enjoying the time that remains. We still have May and June, and then we'll see what happens after that." Kevin squeezed my hand and smiled. "Does your mom still have any of those oatmeal and raisin biscuits *(cookies)* left?"

Chapter Thirty-Nine
Confusion

Hi Amy,

It's really weird for me to think that I'm already a senior and you guys are just finishing up your junior year. Are you going to the junior prom with anyone? Last night the seniors at Lesterford had a dance that's like the prom, but it's called the Matric Ball. Kevin and I went to it with Laura and Spencer--awesome night. First, we went to dinner at a restaurant that had this 100-year-old olive tree growing inside. We all ordered seafood. I heard the chef sails out on his own boat and catches the fish himself, but I don't know if that's true. We got to the dance about 9:00. Lots of fun! See you soon. Can't wait!

Shelly

For the longest time I stared at the end of my email. *See you soon! Can't wait!*

Finally, I pressed the SEND button and it sped into cyberspace. I reached for the phone and dialed Laura. "Hi, what's going on?"

"Not much at this end. Why?"

"The strangest thing happened. I sent an email to my friend, Amy, and at the end I wrote, 'See you soon; can't wait.' But you know, I have mixed feelings about returning home. I shouldn't, but I do. Why's that?"

"Hmm...does it have anything to do with Kevin?" Laura asked.

"Yeah, but it goes further than that. I miss Amy and the rest of the group. They've been my friends for so many years. We've done so much together. When I first heard we were moving here, I freaked out. The life I always had is back there. But now things have changed."

"How's that, Shelly?"

"Like, what about all of you? Will I see you girls again? This place is so far. Why does life have to be so darn complicated?" The tears welled up in my eyes and fell down onto my hand.

"I'm going to miss you too, Shelly. It seems like you've been here forever."

"That's what's so weird. How can friendships grow that quickly?" I asked.

"I think if everything is aligned, they can."

"This semester will be over in a couple of weeks. I need to study for exams but it's hard focusing."

"You'll adjust, Shelly. You know, next year this time *none* of us will be here."

"What do you mean?" I asked.

"Think about it. We'll all be off at different universities making new friends and living through new experiences.

That doesn't mean we can't keep in touch. Maybe someday after college we can have a major reunion."

"That's true. We could do that. I could either come back here or we could meet in the states."

"Yeah, or halfway like in Rio," laughed Laura.

"Now that's an excellent plan. I called you for a reason, Laura. You have this way of making things seem clearer to me."

"Hey, cheer up! I'll see you tomorrow at school."

"Okay...bye."

I got up and fell on my bed. I reached over for good ole Miguel, the stuffed armadillo. I brought him for a reason. "You've been ignored most of this year, Miguel. Sorry about that. I thought I outgrew you. Guess not." As I hugged him, the stress of leaving broke through, and I found myself sobbing into my pillow.

"What's wrong, Shelly?" I jumped up and quickly wiped my face with my sleeve.

"Mom, when did you come in?"

"Just now—I heard you crying. What's wrong?"

"I don't feel like talking about it."

"Can I guess? Is this about returning and leaving your new friends behind?"

"Sort of," I answered. "You know, before we moved to Cape Town I was angry and very nervous. But now things are different. I should be excited about returning to our house and Jackson High, but the reality of it is I'm not."

"I see," answered Mom, "and because of that you feel guilty and confused."

"That's pretty much it."

"You've made some excellent friends here," said Mom. "The difference is when you left the states, you knew you'd be back to finish your senior year with your friends back home. So the move never felt final."

"I know. Leaving here? I don't know if I'll ever be back. I probably won't see any of these kids again."

"That's very possible," said Mom. "But nothing is ever truly lost. Whatever you've learned and whomever you met, bits and pieces will remain with you forever. It's all those experiences that help mold you into the person you'll eventually become."

"But that doesn't help me now."

"You know, Shelly, one thing I've learned is that some friendships last forever, while others last for only a brief time. Why that happens, I don't know. But it certainly doesn't mean these friendships are any less important."

"I don't know what you mean."

"Okay, let's say a friendship had a purpose. Maybe the purpose was to share an experience or to help you get through a tough time."

"Like Laura?" I asked.

Mom looked at me and nodded, "Like Laura."

"But why do things have to be so complicated?"

"Is this also about Kevin?"

I pulled myself up into a sitting position and looked at my mom. I drew a deep breath and said, "That's part of it. I've never had a boyfriend before and when I finally meet someone I can actually tolerate for more than a half hour, I have to leave."

"I know. You both seem to get along quite well, but the reality of it is he lives here and you live thousands of miles away."

"Well, that stinks."

"You both are still young with lots of life's experiences

yet to come your way. Even if it were in the stars to remain here, the probability that you and Kevin would continue to see each other is pretty slim."

"Mom, that's horrible to say."

"Sooner or later, things like college or different goals in life may result in the need for either of you to stretch your wings and fly. And quite honestly, Shelly, you should. You both should."

"I plan on staying in touch with him, Mom," I said trying to convince myself.

"Shelly, I guarantee that if you're meant to reconnect, you will."

Chapter Forty
Sala Kahle, South Africa

Several days ago we shipped back the packed boxes that had occupied the living room. My dad planned to stay behind for another month to finish his work at UCT. I tried to persuade my mom into letting me stay, but the answer remained the same. I guess I'm not surprised.

"Shelly, you have company," Mom announced as she tapped on my bedroom door. I went out to the kitchen and found the girls sitting around the table talking.

"Hi guys, what's happening?"

"We stopped over to say good-bye," said Kim.

"We also have a little gift that all of us pitched in to give you," said Laura handing over this small package wrapped in blue foil paper.

I placed the gift on the table. "I'm going to miss all of you. You have no idea how much your friendship has meant to me."

"We're going to miss you, too," Hannah said.

"But you don't know how nervous I was moving here. Everything I ever knew was back in the United States. If it hadn't been for you girls, I would have been miserable. I've learned so much from each of you."

"Shelly, you're going to make me cry," said Hannah. "You know, we loved having you as a friend. At first, you were the new girl from America, but now you're just Shelly."

"Come on you two, stop all this or I'll be crying, too," Lacey said. "Open your gift, Shelly."

I reached for the gift and tugged at the wrapping paper as slowly as possible with the intent to make this special moment last for as long as possible. Inside was a small, powder blue box. "Is this a piece of jewelry?" I asked.

"Open and see," Laura said as she scrunched the wrapping paper into a ball.

"Oh, wow! Girls! This is so nice." I held up a gold chain that had a flower charm hanging from it. "Is this the protea?" I asked.

"You've learned your flowers," Lacey teased. "We wanted to give you something that would remind you of South Africa."

"We thought the protea necklace would be meaningful because it's South Africa's national flower," added Kim. "Here put it on."

I unhooked the clasp, hung it around my neck, and admired it in the mirror. The flower had a white center that resembled a pin cushion. Several deep crimson flower bracts encircled that center. "It's amazing, absolutely amazing. Thank you so much. I love it!"

"You're welcome," said Lacey.

"Now it's my turn. Wait here." I went to my room and

returned with four small gift bags. "I have something for each of you."

"We're getting a gift? But we're not leaving," joked Hannah.

"I know, but I wanted you to have something to remember me by. They're all the same, so you'll have to open them at the same time. Ready? On the count of three: 1...2...3... open!"

"The Statue of Liberty," all four girls said together as Mom walked into the room and smiled at everyone.

"This statue is located in the state where I live. I thought you might like it. It's to remind you that you have an open invitation to visit me...whenever."

"That would be awesome," said Kim, "going to America."

"Yeah, maybe the four of us could come and visit together," added Lacey.

"I second that invitation," said Mom. "Seriously girls, you'll always have a place to stay. We can make room for all of you."

"Thanks, Mrs. Kilpatrick—that might be the incentive I need to save my money," said Hannah. Her flushed face made her freckles bleed into each other.

"Mrs. Kilpatrick, could you take a picture of us with my camera?" asked Laura.

"Sure, why don't we go out in the backyard and stand by the brick wall."

After the group photo was taken, each of the girls wanted their picture taken with just me. I felt like a celebrity. Laura said she would email the photos to each of us.

"Shelly, Shelly," Mei called out as she ran over to me and tried to say something in my ear.

"Mei, stop whispering. Just tell me."

"Your lovey dovey, Kevin, is here!" she yelled. Hearing that, everyone started laughing.

"Mei, why did you yell that?"

"You told me not to whisper."

"Okay everyone; say he's not standing behind me."

"I'm not standing behind you," said a deep voice. I quickly turned around and saw Kevin. "Looks like you guys are having a party and I wasn't invited."

"We're just leaving, Kevin," Laura said as she winked at me. "See ya, friend." We gave each other the longest hug.

"If ever you decide to come to Jackson High, let me know and I'll be your guide."

"Okay, it's a deal."

After the girls left, Kevin asked if I would like to get a pizza. I quickly changed clothes and put on fresh makeup.

At the pizza shop, Kevin asked, "When do you leave tomorrow?"

"Our plane leaves at 10:30 in the morning. My dad said we have to be in the car backing out of the driveway around 7:30." I looked at him, studying every detail of his face—his blue eyes, dimples, blonde hair. I wanted to remember it always.

"The last few months have really been fun for me, Kevin. I'm going to miss you."

"I wished we met last July when you first got here," Kevin said as he looked down at the table. "All that time was wasted."

I thought about what my mom mentioned earlier and said, "I know but if we had, it probably would be even harder to say good-bye."

"I have something for you." Kevin handed me a nicely wrapped package.

"Did you wrap this?" I asked.

"Nah, the lady at the store did. You don't want to see how it would look if I wrapped it."

"What is it?" I opened up a white box and pulled apart two Styrofoam halves. "Oh wow! I can't believe you remembered how much I like this." Inside was a Raku elephant with a written note attached. It said:

Dear Shelly,

Remember the day you pulled me into the art room to see the Raku animals? You were so excited over them that it was easy choosing something for you to take back to America. I decided to get the elephant because you said it was your favorite. But most of all, elephants are known to have great memories. I'm hoping you will always remember Cape Town and especially me. I'm going to miss you a lot.

Love,
Kevin

I looked up at him and smiled. "This is such a wonderful gift and your note means a lot. Thank you so much."

"Do you really like it?"

"I absolutely love it. You put a lot of thought into this gift. Hey, I have something for you, too." I pulled out a gift bag that sank to the bottom of my backpack.

"What is it? It's pretty heavy," Kevin laughed. As he lifted the bag and placed it on the table, a loud CLUNK could be heard. "Now you have my curiosity!" Slowly he opened the bag and pulled out a chunk of rock.

"Do you know what it is?" I asked.

"Yeah, it's a geode. That's cool—what made you think of that?"

"I got it at the gem store. Actually I bought a whole geode. It looked like this ugly block of concrete until the guy cut it in half exposing all those sparkly, blue and white crystals inside. Isn't it amazing how spectacular the inside is? Wait, I want to show you something else."

I went back into my backpack and pulled out another one. "Here's the other half—I'm keeping that." I picked up Kevin's geode and placed it next to mine. "See how they come together? So whenever I look at my half, I'm going to think of you looking at yours. Do you think that's crazy?"

"No, not at all...actually, I think that's kind of nice. You know, the symbolism and all. Hey, I need to tell you what I've been thinking."

"What's that?" I asked as the waitress put the pizza down on the table.

Kevin scooped out a slice and placed it on my plate and then gave himself one.

"You know how my aunt and uncle live in Philadelphia? Well, I'm thinking about living with them and going to the School of Pharmacy there."

I sat there with the pizza half in my mouth. I almost choked when I heard that bit of news. Quickly swallowing, I stared at Kevin to see if he was serious. Finally I said, "Kevin, I'm applying to Drexel College for journalism."

"Uh huh," he said as he went for a second bite. "I know."

"Drexel's in Philadelphia."

"Really? Now that's one huge coincidence."

"This is surreal! Are you serious? Will your parents go for that?" I asked.

"They're all for it. Actually, they've always encouraged me to go abroad to study as they feel it would be a growing experience. But I think they always thought I would go to a university in Holland. More importantly, Shelly, how do you feel about it?"

"I don't know. Wow! I'm just trying to process all of this. Kevin, I can't think of anything better than both of us being in Philadelphia going to college."

"Timing is everything, you know. Besides, the college in Philadelphia has an excellent school of pharmacy plus it's a great opportunity to get to know my aunt and uncle better. And now, seeing there's a possibility you might be there; hey, I'll look you up!" he laughed.

"Never in my wildest dreams did I expect this would happen," I said shaking my head in disbelief.

"Well, the way I see it, I'll be finished with my senior year in five months. So I'm thinking I could request admission in January in order to get started on some prerequisites."

"Sounds like you've researched this," I said.

"I have. It's on their website. I need to fill out the forms, take the required entrance exams, and check to see how my aunt and uncle feel about having me as a border."

"What if they say no?"

"I don't think that will happen. My cousin graduated from the university last year and is working in Richmond, so I know his room is available. Besides, they like me," he winked.

"I won't be finished with my senior year at Jackson until a year from now. I'll be starting college the following August."

"No problem—I'll be a semester ahead of you. We can see how things work out," said Kevin. "I don't think Pennsylvania is that far from New York."

"Not at all—it's the next state over. This is totally un-believable," I said as Kevin reached over and squeezed my hand. "Kevin, I just hate saying good-bye."

"It's not forever, Shelly. You'll see."

The next morning came too quickly. Dad drove us to the airport as planned; we said our good-byes and found our way to the departure gate. Two hours later we belted ourselves in our seats. Mei sat by the window and watched the activity outside. Mom chose the aisle seat, and I sat in the middle. I heard Mei jabbering about all kinds of stuff, but I blocked it with my own personal thoughts.

"Shelly, you look preoccupied," Mom said breaking my concentration. I decided not to tell anyone about Kevin's plans right yet. After all, it may not happen. Who knows how things might change once I'm gone. He may not even remember me in six months. Someone else could replace me and then there goes the Philadelphia plan.

"Mom, remember the quilt you made Mei before she arrived from China?"

"You mean the Bai Jia Bei quilt?"

"That's the one—all those people sent in a swatch along with a good wish for her."

"Why do you bring that up?"

"I don't know. I remember how I made a square out of my old blanket for Mei and attached that red thread."

"I love my quilt," said Mei. "What's that poem again… you know…about the thread?"

"Actually Mei," Mom explained, "it's an old Chinese saying:

'An invisible red thread connects those who are destined to meet, regardless of time, place, or

circumstance. The thread may stretch or tangle, but will never break.'"

"Today that poem has a double meaning for me," I said staring out the window.

"Why's that?" Mom asked.

I turned and looked at my mom and sister and then said, "Well, first the thread connected us to Mei. But now it's connecting me to my friends in Cape Town."

"You're growing quite a web, Shelly," Mom said pulling a magazine out of her bag. I nodded in agreement and smiled.

Our plane started to back up. After a few minutes, the engines roared and we raced down the runway. I thought back to that day in the kitchen when Dad first told us we would be moving. I was upset. I thought my life was ruined. Dad was right. I have changed. Living in another part of the world and experiencing a different culture has changed me. I hate to admit it but Mom was right, too. I could still hear her voice that day in my room back in New York telling me to just ride the wave. "When you try to buck something you have no control over, all you get is a rough ride," she warned.

I glanced out the window and took my last look of South Africa as the jet gradually lifted off the ground and pointed itself towards America. "Sala Kahle, *(Good-bye)* South Africa," I whispered. I sat back in my chair, closed my eyes, and allowed the plane to take me back to New York.

African Community

African Countryside

Bourke's Luck Potholes

Cable Car to Table Mountain

Cape of Good Hope

Monkey in the Wild

Safari in Kruger

Safari in Kruger Park

Tree Consumed by Termites

View from Kirstenbosch Botanical Gardens

ALSO BY Freddie Remza

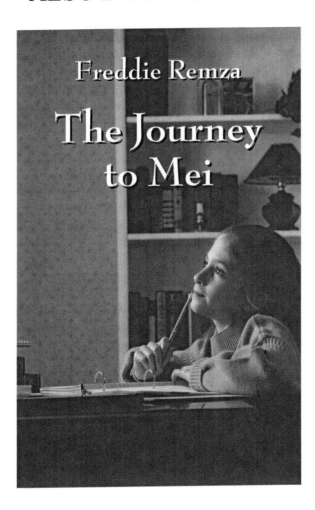

The Journey to Mei

Ten-year-old Shelly is upset when she discovers that her parents plan to adopt a child from China. Shelly enjoys her 'only child' status and is not willing to give it up without a little struggle. As she becomes more aware and lets go of her selfishness, we see her evolve into a caring person anxious to become a big sister to a child far away.

This book is a valuable resource that could be given to the adopted child to read when she's a little older. It's also a story that could be handed to the child's siblings, cousins, classmates, and friends. Actually, with the world getting smaller each year, "The Journey to Mei" could be read by all children to foster an understanding of another country's traditions and culture.

Freddie Remza

"The Journey to Mei" will be a valuable asset to all people adopting from China." Even though we've spoken about some of the issues of adoption when our child was younger, it's nice to see it in a story and to read and discuss it together. The book explains so much and does so very simply, clearly and delicately.

-C. Stasko Mother of an adopted daughter from China

Learn more at: www.outskirtspress.com/ thejourneytomei

Breinigsville, PA USA
29 March 2011
258707BV00004B/18/P

9 781432 766429